MW01614150

SUSAN B. JOHNSON

STARTING FROM ZERO

A NOVEL

2015

Disclaimer

This is a work of fiction. Names, characters, places, and incidents are the product of the author's imagination. Thus, any resemblance to actual persons, living or dead, business establishments, events, or locales is entirely coincidental.

ISBN-13:978-1503219427
ISBN-10:1503219429

To order additional copies, please contact createspace.com, amazon.com, or the author at susan@susanbjohnson.com.

ACKNOWLEDGEMENTS

I am deeply grateful to my husband and first reader, Fred Johnson, whose keen eyes always alert him to errors and absurdities that my own overlook. Much love and gratitude goes to my adult children, Timothy Thompson and Kelly Johnson—always in the cheering section. I'm indebted to the members of Savannah Authors, especially my friend and fellow writer Alice Twiggs Vantrease, who has volunteered hours of her time guiding me down the circuitous path to publication.

SUSAN B. JOHNSON

STARTING FROM ZERO

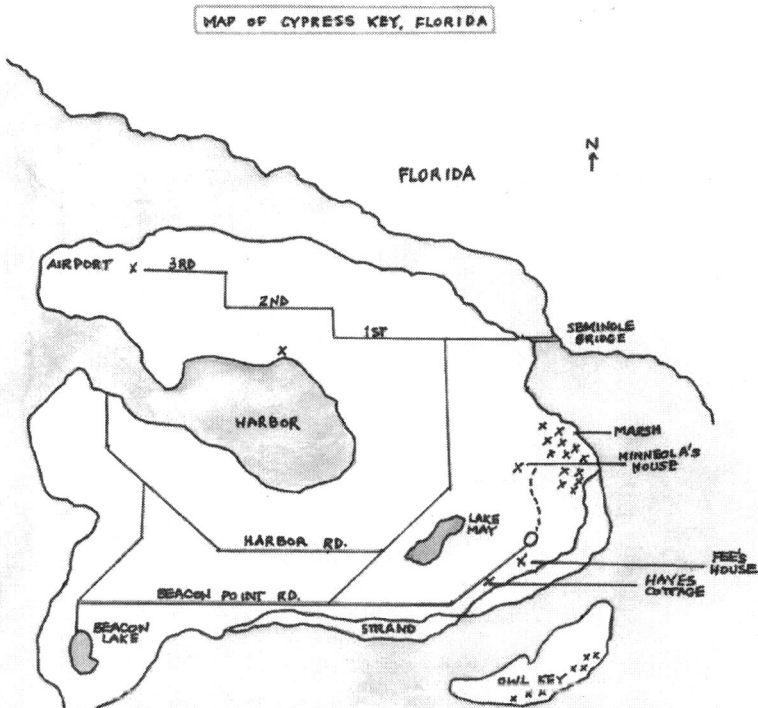

MAP OF CYPRESS KEY, FLORIDA

FLORIDA

N ↑

AIRPORT X 3RD
2ND
1ST
SEMINOLE BRIDGE

HARBOR

MARSH
MINNEOLA'S HOUSE

HARBOR RD.
LAKE MAY

BEACON POINT RD.
FEES HOUSE
HAYES COTTAGE

STRAND

BEACON LAKE

OWL KEY

BEACON POINT

GULF OF MEXICO

Chapter 1
Friday, December 12, 2014

T he first angry winds of December roar southeast from Manitoba, Canada, drink greedily from Lakes Superior and Huron, and spew their wrath along the southern shore of Lake Erie. In Belleporte, Ohio, just twelve miles west of Cleveland, the thermometer plunges twenty-three degrees between the beginning and end of the six o'clock news.

Shoulders hunched, the man shifts from foot to foot, squinting across the dark yard at the house from behind the oak tree concealing him. Cold rain drips from the bare limbs overhead onto his down-filled vest. His body twitches and trembles in response to the chill wind and the drug-starved blood coursing through his damaged veins. A tremor starts in his bowels and ripples upward toward his chest and throat with a chemical urgency as primal as hunger or thirst.

He forces himself to concentrate. No lights on. Sodden newspaper on the flagstone walk. Nobody home. He squints against the rain and blows on his cupped hands. Someday he'll live in a house like this, a big two-story with a wide front porch. He'll have himself a 60-inch T.V., a Ducati motorcycle, and all the crack he wants. It's not right, her owning this fancy place while he has nothing. A fist of anger clenches in his chest, one that he knows can grow and grow until he has to grab something and smash it to keep himself from exploding.

Behind him a movement catches his attention, and his eyes skitter about in the darkness. A dog? He can't be sure. Police? They catch him hanging out in this weather, they'll haul his ass to a jail cell and leave him there to sweat and puke and hope to die. He knows about the agony—from Rollo Guzman and Joystick who've been there.

When a squirrel darts out from beneath a nearby bush, the man flinches, then shivers and resumes his rocking to ease the grinding in his gut, to quell the flashes of green lightning that strobe behind his eyelids. The fingers of his right hand caress the smooth, bone handle of the switchblade. *Good blade, quick and deadly.* He grins and nods in the darkness, grins and nods and rocks against the wind.

His left hand searches his pocket for coins. Two quarters and a dime. Shit. Not even enough for a joint, let alone enough junk to get him through the night. He wipes his nose on his sleeve, then squats, hugging himself to conserve body heat. Nobody can see him here in the darkness behind this tree, but he can see everything—the entrance to the driveway on Winwood Street, the roof of the house next door beyond the tall hedges. Nausea doubles him over, and he fights the urge to lie down, knowing the cold to be an enemy even more deadly than the drug for which every nerve end screams.

He flashes on an image from his boyhood: Sister Mary Agnes, tucking the old quilt around him and smoothing back his hair. But he shakes the thought away. He doesn't need her. Doesn't need anybody. He closes his eyes and leans his head against the oak's rough bark.

Headlights sweep across the yard and swing into position before the garage door—a van whose taillights create plumes of red exhaust in the sodden night air. As the automatic door begins to rise, the man behind the tree pulls his collar up around his ears, snatches a ski mask from his pocket, and pulls it down over his face. Palming the blade, he scuttles to the rear of the vehicle, crouching in the shadows. He follows it into the garage and tenses, careful not to signal his presence with movement or sound. A quick glance around assures him that no other car occupies the second space. Except for some garden tools and an extension ladder, the garage is empty.

For a moment the driver sits nodding her head to the rhythm of a jazz saxophone, her earrings catching and reflecting in the dim light of the dash. When the number ends with a high squeal, she shuts off the ignition while the automatic garage door descends and half-turns to gather parcels from the seat beside her. Then she releases the locks and steps out.

With thudding pulse, the man watches first one shiny black shoe, then the other, descend onto the cement floor. The moment she stands he lunges, knocking her off balance and crooking his right arm around her throat—a slender woman in a bright red raincoat. He speaks gruffly, his voice a hoarse whisper.

"Geddown."

He brandishes the blade in front of her, alert to danger signals. If she starts to scream, he'll tighten his arm across her windpipe and push the point of the blade against her throat.

"Oh God." She hesitates only a moment, her eyes darting wildly about the cold garage; then she drops her packages and goes down hard on one knee. Her panic galvanizes him, and he grins behind the mask, reveling in the surge of power, the rush of absolute control.

Like a lion toying with a rabbit, he loosens his grip, and she tries to crawl away, but her raincoat tangles around her knees. He has her now. Shifting the knife to his right hand, he watches her closely while he fumbles for the zipper at his fly.

"Oh please, no," she whimpers. Her face twists upward, a terrible pleading in her eyes. The mingled scents of fear and perfume galvanize him.

"Shut up," he snarls, swinging his steel-toed boot into the woman's face. The blow spins her around and sends her sprawling, her forehead hitting the cement floor with a thud. Blood gushes from her nose staining the white silk scarf at her throat. When his boot thuds into her side, she grunts once, then lies spread-eagled, her hand still clutching the keys. As the automatic ceiling light clicks off, he mounts her, tearing at her clothes, her unresisting flesh. At last he rolls away, panting, his drug hunger heightened by rage and adrenaline.

By the dim light of the open van door, he gropes for the keys. For a moment he kneels beside her contemplating his next move, the knife point pressed into the soft flesh below the woman's jawbone. Then he slowly draws the razor-sharp blade through her ear lobe and removes the sparkling stone from its hole.

"Move and you're dead," he whispers. He snatches the garage door opener from the dash and presses the "up" button. Then flinging her shoulder bag onto the front seat, the man backs the van swiftly down the driveway and speeds away into the night.

Chapter 2

Saturday, December 13

For one muddled moment, Madelyn Ives thinks she has fallen asleep on the beach, her face stiff and swollen with sunburn. Then the fog lifts, revealing the side table with its aluminum water pitcher, the high narrow bed on which she lies. *Where am I?* she thinks. When an intercom voice pages "Doctor Abrams, Doctor Janet Abrams," she knows she's in a hospital. *My God has the cancer come back?*

She tries to cry out in protest, but her tongue has grown huge and won't form the words. Terrified, she feels for her "good" breast and gasps as pain sears through her left side. In rising panic, she struggles to sit upright.

"Easy, Ms. Ives," says a soothing female voice. "You'd best lie still and let me help you. How about a sip of water?"

Her lips have ballooned, and she can't breathe through her nose. She strains to focus on the woman in white who smiles down at her and lays a cool hand on her forehead. "What's happened to me?"

"You're in Belleporte General, but you're going to be just fine. Here, have some of this." The nurse tries to slip a straw between her lips, but Madelyn knocks it away. "Why didn't they ask me?" she tries to shout, but something presses against her throat, making her voice froggy and weak.

"The doctor will explain. I'll let him know you're awake. In the meantime, please just lie quietly." The nurse tugs at the covers with a firm hand, beckons to a nearby aide, and disappears.

Madelyn's fingers probe her body as her mind gropes for answers. Her right breast is still there, thank God, so what happened? A wreck? Despite the nurse's warnings, she gingerly flexes her ankles, her knees. Everything works—except her right eye, which won't open more than a slit. She sinks into the pillow and feels the blood pounding in her temples.

Was it today that she'd met with her department head? No, her watch says it's Saturday morning, so it was yesterday that they'd lunched in a booth at Ernesto's. Dr. Friedman had not been pleased about her impending leave of absence. Not only would he have to hire staff to cover her three upper-level composition classes, but he'd also be deprived of the opportunity, during their occasional Friday lunch meetings, to press his knee against her thigh. He'd plied her with wine, which she barely touched, while she fended him off with questions about his recent trip to India—a cat-and-mouse game that he enjoyed, she endured, and both recognized as "the way things work."

Afterward, unable to bear the thought of her empty house, she'd shopped at Fein Jewelers, then gone alone to see *Dust and Ashes*. Not at all David's type of film—nor hers either, as it turned out. Her husband would have snorted at the gratuitous sweaty sex and hokey dialogue. By the time she'd slogged through the rain in the theater parking lot, it was after seven and dark. Then what?

A white-coated physician enters the room, stethoscope dangling. He studies her face with professional concentration, then gently lifts each lid to inspect her eyes with a tiny beam of light.

"I'm Dr. Bolger," he says, taking her wrist between his thumb and two fingers.

As she frames her question, she focuses on his clean, squared-off fingernails, the dark wrist hairs that curl from beneath the white sleeve. "What happened to me?"

He fits his stethoscope to his ears and holds the cool metal disk against her flesh. After a moment, his face relaxes. "How do you feel?"

"Like I've been hit by a bus. Have I?"

"Not exactly." He pulls a chair close to the bed and sits, leaning forward, his elbows on his knees. "Last evening a couple out walking their golden retriever found you lying unconscious in your garage. Actually, it was the dog that found you. They called EMS, who learned your name from a credit card in your coat pocket. Do you remember—anything?"

"No." Images and sounds flash across her mind— rain creating halos around street lights, the slap-slap of windshield wipers, Jessica's twentieth birthday bracelet in a silver box on the passenger seat. She'd stopped at Ohio Sam's for a take-out chicken Caesar salad and planned to celebrate her forthcoming sabbatical with supper in the tub.

She remembered lights and sirens and urgent muted voices. People questioned and probed and turned her like a rib roast on a spit. Take a deep breath, exhale. Follow the light, please—up, left, down—that's a girl. Does this hurt? How about this? Let's put your feet in the stirrups, please, this will only take a minute.

Cold metal inside her. Someone scraping debris from beneath her fingernails, then, with an apology, combing her pubic hair. She remembered being propelled on a cart down a long hallway as fluorescent lights strobed by overhead. At some point she soared, hovered near the ceiling, watching a nurse immobilize a woman's head while a young intern with weary eyes took stitch after tiny stitch in her earlobe. Had she dreamed that someone sobbed, calling "David, David?"

"It was dark," she whispers. "Then—."

"Anything else?"

She hesitates, trying to focus her thoughts. First music, then darkness. She could smell him—more acrid than sweat, more rank than fear. A feral odor, an animal on the hunt. "A man!" Her eyes wild, she struggles against Dr. Bolger's restraining hands. "A man in a ski mask. He—my God, what did he do to me?"

"Roughed you up a good bit." His soothing voice cushions the impact of the words. "You have bruised ribs and a laceration of the right ear—nothing life-threatening." He gives her hand a squeeze. "However—"

He sighs, removes his glasses, and tucks them in his breast pocket. "Sorry to have to tell you this," he says, watching her closely. "But I'm afraid there *is* evidence of sexual assault."

Her hands fly to her mouth. "Oh, my God."

"We've already done some tests, and we'll be doing more later this morning. The important thing now is to stay calm and rest to let your body heal." He smiles and pats her knee as if she were a child.

"Am I—torn down there?"

"Only slightly. Dr. Anita Ambrose attended you. You'll be sore for a few days." He glances at his watch, then jots something on her chart. "Not all the news is bad. Initial tests indicate negative HIV."

"AIDS!" Madelyn whispers, horrified. Despite the wracking pain, she rolls onto one side and draws her knees to her chest. Hot tears squeeze from between her swollen lids and slide to the pillow, which abrades her cheek like pumice. How could this have happened?

"First cancer," she says, rocking back and forth. A ragged sob bursts from her swollen throat. "And now this."

From the black emptiness within her, a wail rises to the surface. Her body stiffens, then jerks in violent spasms. She feels strong hands hold her as she thrashes and vomits, her revulsion doubling her physical pain. She doesn't see Dr. Bolger quickly introduce Atavan into her I.V., but she welcomes the darkness that collects her into its vortex and swirls her into oblivion.

Chapter 3
Saturday, December 14

A   t noon Madelyn feels a cool hand on her forehead and forces open her left eye.
        "Feeling better?" asks the nurse. She places a thermometer between her patient's lips, then takes her blood pressure. "Normal," she announces with a smile. "That's good." She adjusts the window blind to let in the gray light, then raises the head of the bed and plumps the pillows. "How about some lunch?" Without waiting for an answer, she wheels a tray table into position. "While you're eating—providing you feel up to it—the police would like to ask you some questions."

Madelyn sags in exhaustion. All she wants is to put last night behind her, release it like a black balloon into the atmosphere. She doesn't want to talk about the assault—not to anyone, and especially not to a stranger.

With effort, she lifts the domed lid covering her

plate: macaroni and cheese, sliced carrots, and green Jello. She averts her face in distaste just as a young man in tan corduroys and a brown ski sweater peers around the edge of the door.

"Okay if I come in?"

He hangs his leather jacket over the back of the visitor's chair and extracts his wallet from a hip pocket, holding it open to display the police badge. "Sergeant Neil Steffan, Belleporte P.D.," he says. "The doc wants me to keep this short." He eases into the chair, flips through the pages of his clipboard, and clicks his ballpoint pen. "What can you tell me about last night?" he asks.

"I was out cold," says Madelyn. "I don't remember anything," She pushes the tray table aside and turns her face toward the opposite wall.

Sergeant Steffan rests his head against the back of the chair and waits. A full minute passes, the silence interrupted only by the whisper of feet in the corridor and a muted voice paging Dr. Kinsky, Dr. Milton Kinsky.

Finally, Madelyn sighs. "He knocked me out and raped me—in that order. That's all I know."

Steffan leans forward. "Ms. Ives," he says quietly, "I'd give anything not to have to ask you questions at a time like this. You didn't deserve what happened to you, and neither will the next person this animal victimizes. My job is to put him away so he never gets the chance, and right now you're the only person who can help me do that." He levels his dark gaze at her. "If you'll give me just ten minutes, I'll be very, very grateful."

Madelyn studies the ceiling tiles, conscious of a caldera of molten rage roiling inside. He's right. She has done nothing to deserve this. For twenty years hasn't she balanced her checkbook, scrubbed toilets, packed lunches? Hasn't she entertained David's clients and served on committees and attended a thousand pointless faculty meetings? What about the stacks of papers she's graded, the lectures she's prepared? Hasn't she carpooled and chaperoned and sat hour after hour in the offices of Jessica's pediatrician, orthodontist, allergist, ophthalmologist? Hasn't she given David back rubs and pep talks and absolute fidelity and the best goddamn years of her life?

What she deserves is a Good Conduct Medal, not an assault by a madman and an insensitive third-degree grilling by some rooky cop! Madelyn clamps her jaw, wincing with the effort. She owes this world exactly nothing, nada, zip. For a long moment the only sound in the room is rain pelting the window glass.

On the other hand, she knows the appalling statistics: that one out of every three women is raped and that the rapist has less than a five percent chance of going to jail. Sergeant Steffan does have a point: She alone can stop him. Otherwise, the next time— God help us, the next time it might be Jessica. She turns wearily toward the man in the chair. "I'll tell you whatever I can."

"Thank you," he says. "What time did you get home?"

"Just after 7:30. It was raining and very dark. I pulled the van into the garage and got out. That's when he jumped me." She hides her shaking hands beneath the sheet.

"A van?"

"Yes, a Ford Freestar. Dark blue." He writes quickly.

"Registered to you?"

"To my husband, David Ives."

He nods. "We'll get on it immediately. I assume you were carrying a purse?"

"Oh God, he's got my keys!"

Steffan extends a calming hand. "Don't worry, we've already secured the house. Describe your purse, please."

"A shoulder bag—black leather with a gold buckle on the flap."

"Money?"

"Not much, maybe twenty dollars."

"Credit cards?"

"Visa, Sears, Shell—I don't remember what else."

"You'll need to cancel those right away—this afternoon if possible." He writes rapidly on his pad, then flips to a clean page. "Describe the man for me, please. Race?"

"White, I think. His face was covered, but I remember his hands. Not very tall—maybe five-ten."

"Age?"

Madelyn hesitates, trying to recall his voice, his body language. "Twenties, maybe. I'm not very good at people's ages."

"Fat? Thin?"

She sorts through an array of images: Charlie Parker on the radio, fear spiking up the back of her neck, an explosion of stars behind her eyes. She shrugs helplessly.

"What about his clothes?" Steffan asks.

"Some kind of jacket—no, a vest—navy blue, I think. One of those quilted things. And a ski mask. Dark blue or black."

He scribbles quickly on his clipboard. "You're doing fine. Did he have a weapon?"

"A knife," says Madelyn. "But I couldn't describe it."

"Long blade? Short?"

"About this long," she says, her fingers spanning six

inches.

"Did he say anything?"

"Yes, he kind of growled at me to get down on the garage floor. He acted scared or excited. And he smelled— an awful smell sort of like—like . . . . I remember being scared for Jessica, my daughter, and what he might do to her." She lies stiffly, willing herself not to crack. "But that was crazy. I knew Jessie wasn't home." Madelyn flinches in pain. "Then he hit me. I don't remember anything after that."

For a moment Sergeant Steffan studies his clipboard, tapping his chin with his pen. "Please think carefully, Mrs. Ives: Who do you know that might want to hurt you?"

The question sucker-punches her, leaving her breathless. To consider that this may not have been a random assault but one for which she bears some responsibility sickens her. Who could hate her so much?

"No one," she whispers.

Steffan glances at the floor between them, then lifts his eyes to hers. "An angry neighbor? Maybe a run-in with someone at work?"

"No, none."

He holds her with his gaze. "Things okay at home?"

Resentment wells up inside her, yet Madelyn knows the question is necessary—one she has to answer. "Despite our separation," she says as neutrally as she can manage, "my husband and I are on friendly terms. He's currently in Amsterdam."

Sergeant Steffan takes his time making note of this information, his expression unreadable. Then he turns to a fresh page. "Any friendships gone sour?"

Madelyn considers, her mind roiling. "Just Vic," she says. "But I'm positive he wouldn't—"

"His full name, please."

Reluctantly, Madelyn complies. "Victor Manolo. We were friends for awhile, but I broke it off a few weeks ago. He didn't take it very well."

"How do you mean?"

"Well, at first he'd call me every night and pretend nothing had happened. After a while when I stopped answering the phone, I'd find him waiting for me outside Stanton Hall—my office at the university."

"Does he work?"

"Yes, at the Tune & Lube on Central."

"How'd you meet him?"

"The van needed service. It took longer than I expected, and he gave me a ride home on his motorcycle. I offered him a beer. We talked." She struggles to keep her tone matter-of-fact. "We became friends."

Steffan frowns. "Are you always so trusting, Mrs. Ives?"

19

SUSAN B. JOHNSON

Madelyn registers the nuance of disapproval in his voice and is tempted to protest that it wasn't the tawdry pick-up he imagines, simply an act of kindness, acknowledged and reciprocated. But she senses that to do so would only deepen his suspicion, so she responds with silence.

"Describe this Manolo," he continues.

"Vic's about your height, well muscled, black hair in a pony tail, tattoos."

"Can you describe them?"

She pictures his forearms, strong and roped with veins. "A flag," she says, "and some kind of creature with wings."

"Where does he live?"

"I asked him once, but he was evasive, so I didn't press."

"What kind of bike?"

"Bike? Oh, you mean motorcycle. Big, black, lots of chrome."

"Why'd you break off with him?"

Madelyn hesitates, sorting out her feelings. "Among other things, he enjoyed making me feel—I don't know, over-privileged and incompetent." *Until the incident with the hatchet.*

How could she explain that Vic's anger at the world

often took the form of taunting, thinly disguised as humor—a weapon too frequently aimed at her. But twenty years with Jessica had prepared her for his mockery—of her speech patterns, her education, her knowledge of literature and art. Her defense, when he would bow and sarcastically refer to her as "the Lady Madelyn" or "Your Grace," she chose to swallow her annoyance and ignore him.

Then one chilly October afternoon she had thrown on a pair of tattered jeans and an old jacket of David's, determined to plant bulbs—tulips and crocuses and paper whites—before the soil in the flower beds hardened for the winter. She had dug up last year's chrysanthemums and had begun to turn over the earth when her spade struck an old forsythia root encroaching on her work space. From the garage she fetched the hand axe and began hacking away, so engrossed in the challenge that she didn't notice that Vic had come up behind her.

"I would have thought all you princesses had lackeys to do that sort of thing," he drawled. "Here, let me."

And suddenly, as if an elastic band had exceeded its stretch, something snapped within her. In one graceful movement she rose to her feet and hurled the ax at a sycamore fifteen feet away. It buried its blade, as she knew it would, while Vic stood by, open-mouthed and speechless.

21

"Thanks all the same," she said, brushing dirt from her hands, "but I can handle it."

Because Vic couldn't bring himself to ask, she never explained how Adam Devlin had taught her to hurl a hand axe during their senior year at Ohio State. How she had practiced that whole semester with a stump as a target until she was nearly as accurate as he. That she could still hit her mark pleased her enormously.

"We both had a lot of unresolved issues, I guess," she says to Steffan.

"And when you told him it was over . . .?"

"He was angry. Got all flushed and started to pace and breathe hard. Smacked the wall a couple of times."

"And then what?"

"And then I got scared and asked him to leave. I guess I thought he might hit me or something."

"And did he?"

"Not really. He gripped my shoulders and shook me a little. Then without another word, he turned on his heel and left." Gingerly, she tents the sheet with her knees. "Look, Sergeant, Vic Manolo's the type who licks his wounds briefly and moves on to someone else. I can't believe he'd hurt me."

Sergeant Steffan glances over his notes, then extracts a card from his wallet and places it on her bedside table.

"Call me if you think of anything else. I wrote my home phone number on the back." He stands. "We've already got some evidence from the scene, so I'm confident we'll find out who assaulted you." He shrugs into his leather jacket, rolling his shoulders and tugging at the sleeves. "By the way, we'll need to keep your clothes for awhile."

"My clothes? Why?"

"The lab will be examining them for blood, hair, that sort of thing."

"Semen?"

"That too. And fingerprints."

"From cloth?"

"Sometimes." He smiles for the first time, a boyish grin that washes the fatigue from around his eyes. "But you leave all that to me." He zips his jacket. "I'll see that your locks are changed and that your new house keys are delivered here this afternoon." He cocks a finger at her. "Your job is to mend." Steffan tucks his clipboard under his arm and leans out the door. "I'm through here," he says to someone in the hall.

A moment later, a tall black woman carrying a Nikon crosses to Madelyn's bedside and offers her hand.

"I'm Willene Herbert, patient advocate," she says. "I rode with you in the ambulance and stayed throughout the initial examination. You and I talked a little last night, but you probably don't remember."

"I don't," says Madelyn, disturbed by the missing pieces.

"How are you?"

"How do you think?"

Unruffled, the woman pulls a pair of half-glasses from her pocket and perches them on her nose. "I'm here to answer any questions you have, although it's a bit early for that; you may still be in shock. Also later on after your bruises develop, I'll need to take some photographs."

"No way," says Madelyn. She squints up at the woman and tries to sound decisive.

"Unfortunately, we need them for evidence," says Willene. "We always wait awhile for the bruises to develop." She smiles down at Madelyn. "But I understand how you feel."

"Wrong!" Madelyn snaps. "You haven't the slightest idea how I feel."

"Good," says Willene. "Anger's good. "You have every right to be mad as hell."

"Don't patronize me."

"First comes shock" she continues calmly, "soon followed by denial. Unfortunately, some women never progress beyond that stage. Believe me, I know. I was one of them." She sits on the edge of the visitor's chair and folds her hands in her lap. "For half a year after I was

24

raped, I tried to just put it out of my mind and go on as before. Merely an unfortunate incident, that's all. Nothing I couldn't handle, right?" She smoothes imaginary wrinkles from her slim gray skirt.

"Then a few months later, the next stage kicked in, and I nearly cracked from guilt and self-loathing. I felt my attack happened because I had dressed provocatively or had behaved irresponsibly. Because I had deliberately put myself at risk, I got what I deserved." Willene opens her purse and withdraws a leather card case. "I really think I might be dead if I hadn't found 'STAAR.' It stands for 'Survivors Taking Action Against Rape.' Every one of STAAR's members has experienced what you're going through right now. They helped me to turn my anger outward, to focus that energy in a constructive way." She places a business card next to Sergeant Steffan's. "They saved my life by teaching me an appropriate way to rage."

Madelyn looks anew at Willene Herbert's perfect manicure, her gray tailored suit. Impossible to imagine this trim, businesslike woman bloodied and violated, pleading for her life on a cold garage floor. *Gritty and filthy. Dirt on the hem of her new red London Fog.*

"No one answered your telephone when I called your house," she says. "Is there someone you'd like me to contact?"

Madelyn struggles to bring some order to her chaotic

thoughts: Contact someone, yes. But who?

Even though David's office will know the name of his Amsterdam hotel, she hesitates to involve him. David is a worrier—especially when it comes to health matters—and will no doubt feel compelled to jump on the next plane and come home. Odd that he, a closet hypochondriac who routinely medicates himself, is always the one with hemorrhoids or post nasal drip while she, who takes nothing but vitamins, is robustly healthy. Except, of course, for cancer which in her nightmares appears in the shape of the shipworm David once told her about, the insidious borer teredo, a shipworm that can honeycomb an entire wooden hull if left unchecked. She would dream that such a worm was feeding on the flesh of her left breast and wake up clawing at her body in horror. But that was then, as Jessica would say, and this is now. Months ago the doctors killed the vermin, cut away the damaged wood, and resculpted her hull, making her as seaworthy as before— until last night, that is.

What can David do that the police and the medical staff can't? Hold her while she cries? Not likely, given their estrangement. Could she stand to have him touch her—so dirtied, so altered by last night's horror? Can he reassure her that Willene Herbert is right, that she hasn't brought this attack upon herself? Won't he silently condemn her for not taking more precautions, not thinking more cleverly, not fighting to the death? She has managed just fine on her own for the last three months, thank you very much. To summon the troops now would signal weakness. No, calling David is not an option.

Although she can hardly breathe, scarcely swallow, she has, after all, lived to tell the tale. "The worst is behind you," her mother announced last March as she perched, ramrod straight, on the edge of a similar hospital chair. "You're a McCandless. It's time to think ahead." True to form, Rose had brought—not a get-well card, not flowers— but the Sunday *New York Times* with the crossword already completed in ballpoint ink. Wrong, Mom, she thinks. If Willene Herbert knows what she's talking about, the worst is yet to come.

But Rose McCandless is halfway to the Caribbean aboard the *Diva* on a month-long cruise. Madelyn's throat aches with edema and unshed tears.

She can't very well call Jessica, who is off "smudging" (whatever that is) on some squalid New Mexico Indian reservation with no hot water, no cell tower, no convenient telephone.

Madelyn knows her neighbor Gil Everhart will drop everything if she calls, will douse himself in "Obsession," and rush to her bedside with an armload of tea roses, determined to hold her hand throughout the night like

27

SUSAN B. JOHNSON

Ronald Coleman in *Winds of War*. Ah, Gil. She loves him dearly, but just now she isn't up to high drama.

Vic Manolo would probably ride to her rescue, but having dumped him, she can't very well ask for his help.

If only Wynn were here, thinks Madelyn. However, as of yesterday her best friend had not returned from settling her mother in a Florida nursing home.

Madelyn squints through her one good eye at the gray window and sighs. That leaves her sister-in-law, Adele, whom she wouldn't call if her hair were on fire.

"Nobody," she says to Willene Herbert, "but thanks all the same."

Chapter 4
Sunday December 14

He remembers the black light lowering inside his head, pressing against the backs of his eyes—the first sign that the locusts have come back. Soon they'd fasten themselves to the edges of his mind and gnaw inward, their whirring faint at first, then gathering strength as they swarmed. Unless he hurried, he knew the sound of the locusts would grow louder and louder until their shrill scream would bring him to his knees. Then he'd start to die, puking and pissing himself and pounding his head against the floor.

He remembers how the flame had hurt his eyes, how he cursed Joystick for taking so long with the spoon, how his hands shook as he yanked his belt tight around his upper arm. Then just as the screaming locusts in his head made him start to drool and gabble with the pain, he grabbed the syringe, flicked it twice to dispel air bubbles, and slid the needle into his vein.

As the feathery caress of the drug descended, he had watched the fire colors spread inward from his fingertips. Weightless and fluid, he rose—away from Joystick and the locusts, through the gray mists, and into the void. He sensed the mounting rush as he rode the beast up through the spinning blackness until suddenly the creature folded its wings, released him, and set him free. And man, did he fly!

Later he remembered the petal softness of female flesh. The way she sat there in the van for a couple of minutes nodding her head to the music of the radio. He searches his memory for the smell of her—flowery like the woods where he used to hide out from Booger Mendel.

Took her sweet time getting out of the van, almost like she was waiting for it, waiting for him. Finally, she shut off the ignition and half-turned to gather parcels from the seat beside her. He had heard the locks release, waited until first one shiny black shoe, then the other touched the cement floor. That's when he lunged, knocking her off balance and crooking his right arm around her throat.

He remembers showing her the blade so she would know not to scream. Just in case, he tightened his arm across her windpipe and pressed the knife tip against her throat. Her panic galvanized him, and he had reveled in the surge of power, the rush of absolute control. Like a lion toying with a rabbit, he loosened his grip then and watched her pivot away, cowering. That's when he knew she was his.

With two fingers he fetches the earring from the watch pocket of his jeans and smiles as its facets catch the light. Not a dumb kid anymore. Not some fucking charity case. Nobody needs to explain to him that when she puts on her pointy shoes and her diamonds, when she sits there rocking and smelling like flowers, she wants it. Oh yes, she wants it.

"Please," she had begged, looking up at him from the garage floor, "don't hurt me." But he knew how her game went. He understood what she really wanted. And so he had played, oh yes.

Chapter 5
Sunday, December 14

At the sound of Wynn Skyler's real voice instead of her recorded one, Madelyn bursts into tears. "Wynn, thank God you're home."

"What's wrong?"

Madelyn forces her voice to stabilize. "Could you— would you be a pal and fetch me from Belleporte General?" she asks. "I'm having a really bad day."

"Oh, Mad, not a recurrence!"

"No, thank God. Please, Wynn, bring me some clothes—something loose like socks and sweats—and get me the hell out of here. I'll explain everything on the way home."

"Give me thirty minutes."

Madelyn's determination to handle matters by

herself had flagged once she remembered she had neither clothes nor cab fare—a déjà vu of a night twenty-five years earlier when she slept sitting on a hard seat in Orly Airport until her luggage—containing her traveler's checks— arrived from London. Now, as then, she waits like an abandoned kindergartner, her mood alternating between frustration and self-disgust.

Although the hospital has provided comb and toothbrush, she has no make-up to help disguise the bruises purpling her eyes and cheek. She has already showered hot and long, scrubbing with as much vigor as she can stand, soaping more gently between her legs. Now she showers again, determined to cleanse away all traces of the attacker's stench, his animal grunts, his terrible presence in her life. She examines the huge magenta contusions blossoming on her thigh and rib cage. Christ, what a mess! Both shins and one knee bear painful scrapes that sting even more in the shower's spray. Grateful for the steam-fogged mirror, she dresses in a clean hospital gown and creeps back into bed, where she waits for Wynn to arrive.

Not until Wynn has helped her into the company truck and slid in beside her does she speak. "You look like shit," Wynn says.

Despite herself, Madelyn laughs. She raises a playful

fist to punch her friend, then freezes in pain. "I can't even bear to look." She huddles in her seat, clutching Wynn's jacket about her shoulders. "Just get me home," she says. "All I want to do is sleep." Without another word, Wynn makes a U-turn and heads for Willow Park on the north side of Belleporte.

Usually Madelyn regards the muddy, leaf-strewn interior of Greenscape's service vehicle with distaste, but today she sinks onto the torn upholstery, grateful to be off her feet and out of the public eye. They ride in companionable silence past gracious old homes rising, like Victorian matrons, from immaculate lawns hedged by boxwood and Raphiolepsis umbellata. The serenity of her neighborhood calms Madelyn, gives her courage.

"I was assaulted last night," she says finally.

"So I gathered."

"In my garage."

"Jesus. Have you talked to the police?"

"Yes, a Sergeant Steffan came by this morning to ask me a lot of questions I couldn't answer—like what was the man wearing and do I remember anything about the weapon. I told him all I know—that a man in a ski mask held some kind of knife at my throat, then knocked me out and stole my purse."

"What's the damage?"

"Scrapes and bruises. Oh yes, and a sadistic little

slice in my ear lobe. What he wanted was a diamond earring; what he got was a thirty dollar zirconium." She turns her cheek to show Wynn the stitches.

"Any money?"

"About twenty bucks. And my cell phone, of course. And credit cards, which a victim advocate helped me to cancel. And Jessica's birthday present, a gold chain worth about $200. And the van. God, David will have a stroke about the van!"

"Anyone notify him?"

Madelyn leans against the head rest and closes her eyes. Madelyn has told Wynn about the suspicions and recriminations, the tears and denials, the words hurled like grenades. She is the only one of Madelyn's friends who knows the separation is not merely another of David's frequent business trips for Kohl & Sumner.

"He's still in Holland," she says. To her chagrin, a single tear rolls down her cheek and onto the collar of Wynn's purple windbreaker. "So there's hardly any point." Gingerly, her tongue explores her swollen lower lip.

"So this reptile took your keys?"

"Yes, but yesterday Sergeant Steffan had my locks changed." She dangles her new keys for her friend to see.

Wynn glances sideways at her. "What happened to your clothes?"

For a moment, the question hangs in the space between them like sewer gas. Clear the air, says Madelyn's voice of reason. Tell it first to Wynn, who won't judge you. But she shrinks from the telling, for to give it voice is to make rape real—a predator like cancer that has crept upon her in the dark to alter her life forever. She can't form the words.

"Ruined," she says at last.

Skillfully, Wynn navigates around bumps and potholes and awkward, probing questions, stopping in front of a house not far from Madelyn's own. A long driveway, partially blocked by another Greenscape vehicle, leads back through the trees.

"Give me two minutes," she says. "I've got to check on this job, which is costing me a fortune in overtime." She increases the heat a notch, keeps the engine running, and hurries off to speak with a workman raking debris into a pile. Madelyn watches him scoop up twigs and leaves and dump them into a wheelbarrow.

Normally, she enjoys the colors and brisk weather of late autumn and winter, but this year's recently completed fall quarter exhausted her as never before. While she enjoyed the preparatory reading for her Advanced Composition and World Literature classes, she begrudged the arduous hours spent composing lectures and evaluating student papers. More than once she fought off the temptation to dump the lot, ungraded, into the recycle bin.

What's more, unless David has a change of heart about what they euphemistically call "the arrangement," or Jessica falls out of love with the Navajo, or her mother, Rose, cuts short her cruise, she will spend Christmas alone for the first time in twenty-two years.

Through the dirty windshield, Madelyn watches Wynn and the workman in conversation, their breath visible in the chill December air. Wynn gestures with a sweep of her right arm as the man nods and wipes his forehead with a bandanna pulled from his back pocket. How does Wynn do it? she wonders. Hard, physical labor. Grueling hours. Living alone all these years with no trace of bitterness or regret. *While I have checked off every one of the 110 days since David left.* She pushes the idea away.

Not until the man turns to watch Wynn walking back toward the truck does Madelyn recognize Cory Neale, Jessica's former classmate. In the two years since she's seen him, his neck and torso have thickened, his arms become muscular. No more the gawky teenager who pursued Jessie, writing her notes and telephoning and following her home from school until finally she shrieked at him, threatening to go to the police if he didn't leave her alone.

Madelyn recalls her ambivalence. Part of her

mistrusted Cory while another part ached for the lonely boy, whose skinny body and geeky guffaws targeted him as a victim. How brutally Jessica had toyed with him— enticing him with moist lips and lowered lashes, then ridiculing him for responding. But Madelyn had not interceded, for she knew that to do so would only encourage Jessica's cruelty. Instead, to compensate, she had paid Cory for cutting grass and washing windows. She didn't object when he trailed after her as she vacuumed or when he perched on a kitchen stool while she peeled potatoes. Not, that is, until the day she emerged from the shower wrapped in a towel and found Cory sitting on the edge of her bed. After that, she limited him to outdoor projects; thank God, he seemed to get the message.

If Jessica were to see this hard-working young man, his shoulders hunched against the cold, would she regret her teenage cruelty? Would she respect him as field manager of Greenscape and part-time handy man? Or would she continue to revile him just for the mean-spirited fun of it all? Madelyn sighs, pulling the collar of Wynn's jacket up around her face. One never knows with Jessica.

As for herself, in a world infested with creeps and predators, the sight of Cory leaning on his rake reassures her of the very ordinariness of her neighborhood where violence does not—cannot—happen.

And yet it has.

What's more, she knows first hand that not all violence is sudden. Sometimes it is slow and insidious like the invasion of her left breast by cancer. During the first few months following her surgery, she would sometimes dream that such a worm was feeding on her flesh and would wake up in horror, clawing at her body.

But that was then, as Jessica would say, and this is now.

She shifts uncomfortably on the front seat, remembering the Ides of March just nine months ago when she had watched Dr. Khroner's eyebrows sliding up and down his forehead as he laid out her options.

"Radicals are rare these days," he had said, "unless there is intense involvement." His terminology, suggesting a political uprising in a third-world country, had momentarily confused her. It was, after all, years since she maintained an "intense involvement" in anything except her family and her job. But when Dr. Khroner reached for her hand, the simplicity of the gesture released an avalanche of crushing comprehension. It was a pivotal moment—one that henceforth would divide her life into "before" and "after." Three days later, her left breast was gone forever.

Her first response was to reject the concept of any future longer than a week. Distracted and depressed by the assault on her body, she allowed all magazine subscriptions to lapse. Houseplants drooped and died of neglect. She did not renew her season ticket to the Cleveland Symphony, and she skipped her dental appointment in May. After all, what was the point?

She emptied the freezer and started shopping daily for groceries like a tourist occupying temporary quarters. At night, sleepless and sweating, she focused inward searching for the enemy as if, like some sci-fi creature, it could be vanquished by the laser of her mind.

After two months, as the ache in her chest and left arm receded, she began to breathe the rarefied air of possibility. In July, at David's urging, she ordered new drapes for the den, and in August she gave a small, elegant dinner party for David's clients, Jane and Bill Blackwell. Her September 12 birthday note to Wynn surprised them both: "Only twenty-two more years until we can retire at 65!"

Thirteen weeks ago, she began the fall quarter with a new canvas briefcase from L.L. Bean, a new desk lamp for her office, and a whole new wardrobe to accommodate her loss of fifteen excess pounds.

Her eager anticipation of a winter leave served as even further proof of her renewed confidence in a full and fruitful life. That is, until the night before last. She shakes away her thoughts as Wynn slides in beside her.

"Never go into the landscaping business," she says with a sigh. "You end up doing every goddamned thing yourself. By the way, I hope you don't mind that I've asked Cory to stop by your house when he's finished here and replace that burned-out bulb in your security light. We'll both sleep a lot better tonight."

"So you'll stay over?"

"Do you really have to ask?"

Fifteen minutes later Madelyn is settled in the corner of her own sofa, an afghan tucked around her knees. Wynn hands her a mug of tea, then rubs her hands together. "Now here's the plan," she says. "You're going to stay put and rest while I go fill the tub."

"Why?"

"So you can soak away those aches and pains."

"No, I mean—why has everything all gone wrong— the plans, the dreams?" *Images: David shaving in their "honeymoon" shower at the Casa de Lobo, his chin upraised, his blond hair plastered against his forehead. Thanksgiving dinner with Jessica squirming in the old McCandless high chair, her chubby arms slick with saliva and dill pickle juice. The three of them tickling each other in the hammock at Little Bass Lake.* She tilts back her head in order to see beneath swollen eyelids.

"Last Christmas I remember thinking how well my

life has turned out. Good health, a close family, comfortable circumstances, a job I like. And then—" She holds on tight, steadying her voice, which wobbles like a loose wheel. Tears well up as she presses both hands against her mouth. She attempts to stem the sound that rises from within like the wail of a wounded animal. But shock and grief and outrage will no longer be denied. A deep shudder grips her shoulders as she sags against the cushions, her fists clenching and unclenching against her damaged face.

"I didn't even know until they t-told me! I didn't even know!" More and more violently she shakes, her head thrashing from side to side, her breath coming in spasms. "He—he—the filthy bastard raped me!"

Swiftly, Wynn kneels beside Madelyn and enfolds her friend's rigid body in her arms, dismayed by the shock of it, the damage, and the depth of Madelyn's need.

"Let it out, Mad," she says as calmly as she can. "Just let it all come out." Like a parent with a wounded child, Wynn rocks her, holds her tightly until her sobbing eases and she sags against Wynn's shoulder.

When it is finally over, Madelyn blows her nose on Wynn's clean handkerchief and lies back on the pillows. "Sometimes," she says, "I think I'm going crazy."

"Balls," says Wynn. "You may, in fact, be the only truly sane person I know. And one of the strongest. But, dear girl, even Joan of Arc must have lapsed now and then." She helps Madelyn stretch full length on the couch and tucks the afghan around her feet.

"This may not be the time to ask," says Wynn, brushing the hair away from Madelyn's damp brow, "but have you dumped the Italian stallion yet?"

"Not very effectively, I guess." Madelyn sighs.

"Poor Vic."

"Meaning—?"

"Meaning he doesn't like to lose. I tried as gently as I could to explain why I can't continue to see him, but he took it pretty hard. Now I think he's following me. Last Thursday after class, I saw his truck parked in front of Stanton Hall. I ducked out the back and came home."

"I never did understand that relationship."

"It wasn't a relationship, just a brief attraction. I was lonely, and he's so different from the other men I know."

"You've got *that* right. Tattoos and motorcycles! Maddy, the man doesn't even speak standard English. How on earth did you communicate?"

Madelyn manages a smile. "Don't be cruel, Wynn. Vic Manolo may be rough around the edges, but he's no dummy. He reads everything—Melville, Hemingway, Dickens. Even a little poetry." But she recognizes that this was only part of the attraction. The rest was his feral instincts, his daring, predatory approach to life. A taker by nature, Vic's currency was charm, and he used it as deftly to deflect street punks as to manipulate bosses and bankers. He viewed every woman as a red cape to his horns, every competitor as an Everest. That Vic was dangerous compelled her and excited a hunger she hadn't known she possessed. She had craved the risk, the rush of the road less traveled. Giving up Vic has been like kicking a habit; even now she feels the pangs of withdrawal.

"Well, I'm glad it's over," Wynn says. "I never trusted him, especially after he roughed you up."

"It was only that one time. We had a silly argument, and he lost his temper. When he realized he had hurt my arm, he felt terrible and kept apologizing over and over. The whole thing was a stupid misunderstanding."

"And that incident didn't ring any alarm bells with you?"

Gingerly, Madelyn shifts to a more comfortable position. "Okay, so he scared me a little. That's one reason he's history."

Wynn picks at a hangnail, avoiding Madelyn's eyes. "I don't suppose," she says quietly, "that he could have been the one who . . ."

"No way," says Madelyn. "His pride may have taken a hit, but I just can't believe he'd—anyway, I'm sure I would have recognized his voice. Please, I don't want to think about it."

When the telephone rings, Wynn hands her the cordless receiver.

"Hello?" Madelyn says. "Hello?" Her shoulders tense as she listens to the silence. "Who is this?" she demands, her voice rising. Suddenly, she drops the telephone as if it were white-hot. "Nobody's answering," she whispers, her face ashen. "But I can hear breathing."

Wynn picks up the phone and listens, then presses the "off" button. "Probably just pranksters," she says, affecting nonchalance. "You know kids. Now how about that bath?"

"First check the doors again, will you, Wynn? Especially the one at the top of the basement stairs." She hears the panic rising in her own voice and struggles to calm herself. Wynn has promised to stay the night, and for that she is very grateful. But as she stares at the wall of family photos—David with baby Jessica on his shoulder; her mother, Rose, in a floor-length red dress; herself in cap and gown—she doubts she'll ever feel safe here again.

Wynn returns a few moments later with an envelope in her hand. "Found this on the floor beneath the mail slot," she says. "Must have been hand delivered."

Madelyn studies the plain white #10 with no stamp, no address, then tears it open and unfolds the single sheet of white paper. She reads:

You walk along a lonesome road
You walk in fear and dread,
because you know a frightful fiend
doth close behind you tread.

Like a blow to the solar plexus, recognition leaves her breathless. She knows the reference well, for not only has she taught the "Rime of the Ancient Mariner" in at least twelve different literature classes, but the poem is Vic Manolo's favorite. She can see him now, strutting back and forth across this braided rug reciting Coleridge with grimaces and melodramatic gestures. She had thought him amusing then, laughed at his antics. Why had she seen only his charm and not his craziness? What a fool to allow him into her life!

She hands it to Wynn, her eyes huge with alarm.

"From Vic," she whispers.

"How do you know?"

"It's his favorite poem, deliberately misquoted."

"This gives me the creeps," says Wynn. "We need to call the police."

Sergeant Steffan is "temporarily unavailable" when Madelyn calls the station, so she leaves her name and number. Ten minutes later her phone rings.

"Neil Steffan, Ms. Ives. You called?"

"Yes, I thought you should know that at some point within the past couple of hours, somebody slipped a threatening note through my mail slot. There's no signature, no return address, nothing."

"What does it say?"

"It's in the form of a poem, suggesting that I'm being followed and by a 'fearful fiend.'"

"Any idea who might have written it?"

Madelyn hesitates, loath to implicate Vic in case she is mistaken. But Wynn is right—there's something sick about this. Maybe, angered by her refusal to see him, Vic has upped the ante. "Possibly the man I told you about, Vic Manolo."

She hears a page ripping from a spiral notebook, the squeak of an office chair. "Okay," Steffan says. "Don't handle the note. I'll be over in the morning to take it to the lab for analysis." He clears his throat. "You, uh, there by yourself?"

"No, my friend Wynn's staying overnight with me."

"Good," he says. "That's good.

Madelyn hears the slam of a metal file drawer. "Get some sleep, Ms. Ives" he says. "And rest assured, we're keeping a close eye."

At 1 a.m., Madelyn hugs her knees in the queen-sized bed, her right cheek against the pansied pillow case. In the dark, the room has an unfamiliar, disturbing glow, the result of the new security light. While Madelyn is grateful to Cory Neale for doing the job so promptly, part of her rebels against the need for such measures. She and David chose this house, after all, for the very purpose of its privacy, the seclusion of its garden amid this community of gracious old homes. But another part of her—the part that trembles when someone breathes into the telephone, that catches herself listening for intrusive sounds—regards darkness as the enemy.

Easing out of bed, she limps down the long hall to the kitchen, hugging her arms against the chill. She pauses to listen to the silent house, relieved when she hears only the hum of the refrigerator, the wail of a distant siren. From the cutlery drawer, she selects a six-inch boning knife with a sturdy wooden handle and tests its point against her fingertip. Then quietly so as not to disturb Wynn in the guest room, she hobbles back to bed and slips the blade beneath David's pillow.

49

Chapter 6
Monday, December 15

Adagger of morning sunlight inches across Madelyn's pillow, piercing her restless dreams. She raises her head to glance at the clock, then falls back with a sigh. Eight o'clock—nine hours since the last telephone call from "the breather." About the fifth time it happened, Wynn abandoned her prankster theory and made Madelyn promise to notify Sergeant Steffan when he comes to pick up the note. Then she unplugged the phone so they could both get some sleep.

But even in the silence, Madelyn can hear the threat implicit in the rise and fall of that breathing: *I'm here, and I'm coming back.*

Several times during the night, despite her friend's reassuring presence in the guest room, Madelyn jerked awake in terror of the dark shape she imagined hovering

SUSAN B. JOHNSON

over her preparing to slice her with his blade. Now she lies exhausted, her body protesting at even the tiniest movement.

She wears a flannel nightgown and a pair of David's wool socks as she keeps to his side of the bed near the bathroom. Rumpling only half, she tells herself, means saving time in the morning. But she knows this isn't the only reason. Part of her hopes David will slip in beside her as she sleeps—assuming, of course, she can manage to sleep at all.

Careful not to wrench her ribs, she pulls on jeans and a loose sweater and limps to the kitchen to make herself a pot of decaf. There she finds the coffee already brewed and a note scotch-taped to the refrigerator:

Hope you got some sleep and are feeling better. In checking my calendar I remembered our lunch date at DiYanni's—12:30 tomorrow. Although I think it would do you good to come, I'll understand if you want to cancel. Just give me a call.

Gotta run. Wynn

Her first thought is, I can't possibly go. But she knows Wynn is right. The sooner she resumes her life, the further she can distance herself from this terrible experience. From a corner of the freezer she pulls a pack of Marlboros and lights up, holding in the smoke until her

52

lungs ache—her first cigarette in eight months. What if David decides to come home for Christmas? She tallies both sides of the ledger in her mind. On the plus side, his presence might forestall further telephone harassment, as well as any nasty gossip about their estrangement. But on the minus, she isn't so naive as to think mere separation has resolved their differences, especially since David's associate Tee Kemball, with whom he insists he is *not* having an affair, still travels with him. Although she has no proof, Madelyn's gut instinct tells her otherwise. She sighs, certain only of one thing. The more she thinks about spending the holidays by herself, the more ambivalent she feels: She'll gladly forego false jollity and the tedious Kohl and Sumner office party in exchange for a quiet Christmas in front of the fire; however, once the sun goes down, every hour she spends alone in this house seems like five.

Until the teredo, she hadn't smoked since college. But under the strain of last spring's fear of disfigurement— or worse, death—she sought comfort from an old habit that David abhored. Like a naughty child, she would puff away in the garage, hiding her pack of cigarettes inside a terra cotta pot.

Disgusted with herself, she flushes the butt into the garbage disposal, then perches on a kitchen stool to open Friday's mail. On the reverse of an aerial-view post card of

Jamaica is a message from her mother: "Everyone has mal de mer but me. Love, Rose M." Madelyn sighs. *Did I really expect hugs and kisses?* She slits open a purple envelope bearing Jessica's bold backhand and pulls the greeting card from within: "Hope you enjoyed my last letter," it says. "Of course, I was much younger then!"

You've got that right, thinks Madelyn. How long has it been—three months? four?—since Jess wrote to say she has "discovered" herself while living among the Navajo.

With effort Madelyn bends to retrieve a photograph that has fallen to the floor and studies the face of her only child, upturned in adoration toward a dark-eyed man with Willie Nelson braids. Judging from the color in Jessie's cheeks, the girl is healthy enough. Despite her itinerant lifestyle, her history of inappropriate friendships, her blatant rejection of middle-class comfort, she looks relaxed and happy—even a bit tan with a hint of sunburn across her short, straight nose.

But an inner voice warns Madelyn against too much optimism. After surviving twenty years of tantrums and mood swings, of lies and rebellion, Madelyn is not about to let down her guard. She loves this girl with all her heart, but she has learned not to invest much faith in surface appearances. No one knows better than she how the angel of one moment can turn demonic the next.

A wave of loss washes over her as she remembers the fear and wonder of giving birth. She hears lullabies and Christmas carols and Milli Vanilli singing "Blame It on the Rain." In the dark corners of her mind lurk ghastly images: the twisted wreckage of the Twin Towers; families clinging to rooftops in Katrina's wake; the terrified eyes of Haiti's orphaned children. But always, always she has swaddled her child in safety, protecting her as best she can from barbs and betrayals and bogeymen.

In the end, none of it matters—not the bedtime stories, the dancing classes, or the summers at Little Bass Lake. Even repeated sessions with Dr. Feingold have made not a whit of difference. Through it all, Jessie has remained hostile and remote as if beneath the simplest act of compliance hums a red-hot current of contempt.

Madelyn jumps at the sound of the front door chimes. She checks the peephole, then releases the chain and deadbolt. Neil Steffan steps forward and hands her a package wrapped in brown paper.

"Your purse," he says. "Couple of kids found it in a culvert over near Lakewood. Your wallet too. Driver's license, pictures, even credit cards, which I assume you've already cancelled. Check to be sure, but I think it's all there except the cash. Unfortunately, the only prints we got are yours and those of the kid who found it." Steffan is wired, jittery. For a moment, he stands at the window pulling his chin, his attention on the tall oak in the front yard.

"There," he says with a little nod at the tree. "Right there's where he hid before ducking into the garage behind you—I'll bet a hundred bucks."

She looks where he points, at Jessie's "hide and seek" tree, and to her chagrin, she feels a lump forming in her throat.

"Don't forget to call your insurance agent," Steffan says. "With a little luck, you'll at least get a new car out of this deal."

"Luck isn't my strong suit these days."

He runs impatient fingers through his hair. "Where is it?"

Madelyn hands him the paper enclosed in a plastic sandwich bag and watches him read, his eyebrows bunching in the center of his forehead. For the first time she notices a scar above his left eye—a thin white line that parallels his eyebrow, then curves upward to his hairline. A knife wound? The rational part of her is grateful that those traumatic seconds had not cost him his sight; otherwise, he wouldn't be here offering reassurance and protection.

"It's part of an 18th century poem" she says, "dealing with the supernatural punishment of a seaman for a thoughtless crime against nature." Even to her own ears, she sounds like some prissy English teacher explaining Coleridge to a teenager.

Sergeant Steffan paces back and forth, pausing only to draw the drapes across the front windows. "Other than Manolo," he says, "who do you associate with this poem?"

"Nobody," she says." Then suddenly a thought occurs: Joe Haven, the weird student from several semesters back. He had turned in a poorly written term paper on "The Raven," a rambling analysis—not of the poem's structure and imagery as assigned—but of its irrefutable evidence proving Poe was possessed by Satan.

She can still see him standing at her office door, his motorcycle helmet in one hand, his backpack in the other.

Can I wait while you grade it?

Afraid I don't have time right now.

You don't like me, do you?

Of course I like you. What makes you think such a thing?

I need at least a C in order to pass.

You'll have your paper back on Monday.

When she did read the paper, she found its premise so disturbing that she considered referring him to a counselor. In the end she gave his work the "F" it deserved along with a reminder that she was "available" should he wish to discuss the grade. Shortly thereafter anonymous telephone calls began at her home. Madelyn remembers icicles spiking down from the eaves of Stanton Hall, hears again the clang of her office radiator. Had she mishandled that whole episode?

"A couple of semesters ago, I had to fail a student, a troubled kid who wrote terrible poetry and hung around my office. His real name was Joe Haven, but one of the students dubbed him 'Poe's Raven,' and the name stuck."

"Go on."

She tells him how bullies were drawn to Raven like sharks to chum, how one night they duct-taped him to a toilet in the library, where he stayed for several hours until he was discovered by the cleaning service and released. Another time they printed his name on an obscene poem and scattered copies all over the campus. But the worst was when somebody slipped Rohypnol into his Dr. Pepper, then dropped him off in a field about five miles from campus without his jeans. The police picked him up and drove him home.

"Turns out he lived alone in a rooming house in Bay Village." Madelyn presses her fingers hard against her throbbing temples. "He changed after that."

"Changed how?"

"He became kind of—sinister. Followed me around campus, giving me the evil eye, almost as if he held me responsible for his unpopularity. I'm pretty sure it was

Raven who wrote 'devil bitch' in the dust on my fender. My husband said I should alert the Dean, but I just couldn't bring myself to do it. Fortunately, the semester ended a few weeks later, and everyone left for winter break. Raven never came back."

"And you haven't had any contact with him since?" Steffan asks.

"No, but for about three weeks after the end of that semester, someone would call our house several times every evening, hanging up if David answered, staying on the line and breathing audibly if I picked up." Madelyn sinks into a chair, her face ravaged by fatigue. "And last night those calls started up again. Five of them between six and eleven."

Steffen jots something on his notepad. "Does the caller say anything?"

"No, he just breathes." She wipes her clammy hands on the arms of the chair. "I've made up my mind to request an unlisted number."

The vertical lines deepen between Steffan's eyes. "No, don't," he says. "It's important that we keep the lines of communication open so I can have the telephone company assemble a report of incoming calls. For the next ten days, if the offender dials from anywhere other than a public telephone or cell, Ohio Bell can immediately determine the owner of that number." He snaps his fingers.

"Better than caller I.D."

"You mean I have to endure this harassment for the next ten days? Why ten days?"

He shrugs. "Phone company policy. Should give us enough time to see if he's going to tip his hand."

She drops her head into her hands. "I don't know if I can stand it," she says, dangerously close to tears.

Steffan assesses her pallor, the tremor in her voice, then faces her squarely. "Tell me, Ms. Ives. Which neighbor do you trust with your house key?"

"That would be Gil Everhart. Next block, gray frame, number 126."

Steffan makes note of this, then jams his pencil over his ear. "Look," he says firmly. "Just to be on the safe side, I want you out of here for a few days. Arrange to stay with a friend—only be sure to let me know where to reach you."

The knot of apprehension, loosened by his presence, tightens once again. "But—"

"Tomorrow."

"If you really think—"

He nods. "I really think."

Chapter 7
Monday, December 15

L ast night he cried again. Had a dream about the scene in the garage, how he pushed her to the floor and tore at her clothes. Woke up with his stupid thumb in his mouth and cheeks all wet just like when he was a little kid, scared that Mama would beat him again if he got out of bed. All night he'd lie there, paralyzed with terror that she'd come home smelling like sweat and want him to touch her body, to put his mouth—

After they took mama away, screaming and bleeding from the razor cuts, he didn't cry for two years. Not until Booger Mendel dragged him to the showers and made him swallow piss. Spent the night puking out his guts on the tile floor, with his hands lashed behind him and his body on fire from the bar of soap duct taped up inside. That was the most pain he had felt since the first time Mama used the handle of the toilet plunger. *Mama, stop!* he had cried, but she just kept plunging it into him until finally the locusts came and whirred him into blackness.

Where the hell's the candy man? Supposed to be here an hour ago. Don't Rollo know how I need?

She acted real scared that night in the garage. He liked it that she was scared, liked the rabbity way her eyes looked when she said, *Please don't hurt me!* He grins and rubs his hand over his chin. *Beard coming in good.*

If that candy man don't get here with the shit in five more minutes, fucking Rollo's gonna hear about it.

Chapter 8
Tuesday, December 16

Kneeling on the hard soil, Madelyn snips away dead blooms on the chrysanthemums, leaving only brown stalks spiking up from the flower bed. She is perspiring from her efforts, even though the night has turned cold enough to show her breath. She shivers, realizing she should have dressed more warmly, or at least worn shoes. Her hand cramps from the clippers, and she lays them aside to flex her fingers and shake away the pain. One sleeve of her nightgown is torn—thin shreds of gauze fluttering like pennants in the night wind—and she knows Mother will be angry at her carelessness. As she gathers her skirt to stand, the gown falls away, leaving her body naked and pale. She starts toward the house, then remembers the clippers and turns. A scream clogs her throat, for he is there behind her, the malodorous monster in the black mask, shuffling toward her, clutching the clippers. Horrified, she tries to run, but her legs have turned to stone. She trips over her own feet and sprawls headlong into the dirt.

"Help!" she cries in panic. Like a wounded animal, she drags herself across the floor to the bathroom, where she awakens clinging to the toilet, her pajamas damp with sweat. When the dream images finally recede, she lowers her head to her knees and weeps in exhaustion. Sergeant Steffan is right, she thinks. I've got to get out of here.

She heaves herself to her feet and turns on the bathroom light. Cupping her hands beneath the faucet, she bathes her red-rimmed eyes, then leans toward the mirror to inspect her face. Some of the swelling on her left cheek has receded, and the magenta rings around her eyes have begun to turn to yellowish green.

Wrapping a blanket around her like a shawl, she sits in the chair by the window, watching rain gully down the glass. It reminds her of a long ago picnic on the floor of David's and her first apartment. It had rained then too, a torrent that flooded her with delight at the thought of their child-to-be. In that moment she had loved David for reasons of gallantry and goodness and honor, knowing him to be steadfast like a lightship on station, equal to any challenge their future might offer. Yet not until months after their wedding had she fallen totally, rapturously in love.

"I lust you," she would whisper, her tongue exploring the outer rim of his ear.

"Not again!" he would whimper, tugging at the elastic on her maternity jeans. Whatever had happened to the simple joy of being together? To the rhythm of easy lovemaking?

The teredo happened, thinks Madelyn bitterly. The worm turned. She closes her eyes against the headache that pulses at her temples. Sergeant Steffan was insistent that she pack up and get out *today,* so tonight she has agreed to bunk at Wynn's. Maybe there she'll feel safe enough to sleep without terrifying dreams.

She draws the blanket up like a hood and settles deeper in the chair. The problem is, despite her friend's protestations, Madelyn can't impose for more than a day or two. Wynn's guest room is also her office, making long-term company out of the question. What if a week goes by and Steffan still hasn't solved this case? Like the rain, tears spill down her cheeks. Where on earth can she go?

"L-G-O-V-P," says Madelyn. "Or maybe that last one's an 'R.' Is it an 'R'?"

"It's an 'R,'" says Dr. Pritchard. "Can you read the next line?"

"Not even when I squint."

He slips a lens in front of her right eye. "How about now?"

"Better," says Madelyn. "So what do you think?"

Frowning, Dr. Pritchard studies his patient. "I think that's one very nasty bruise." He tilts her face upward into the light. "A fraction closer and you might have lost an eye." He hands her a prescription and clips his gold pen to the pocket of his lab coat. "Let me know if reading glasses ease those headaches."

Madelyn drops off her prescription at Opti-Options and looks about for another cab. When none appears, she considers taking a bus, but she has no idea how much change she needs, much less which bus to catch. The prospect of breathing stale public air decides the matter: She will walk the seven blocks to DiYanni's Ristorante, her bruised rib notwithstanding. She sets off slowly down Harding Boulevard, glad to be wearing dark glasses and comfortable shoes.

With thirty minutes to kill before meeting Wynn for lunch, she stops at Fuller Camera to check out the latest photography magazines. Ever since childhood, she has delighted in Fuller's the same way her father used to love Billy's Bait and Tackle. As always her fingers itch to touch the sleek black lenses in the glass display case. She inspects the camera bags displayed along one wall and scans an article on telephoto lenses in the December issue of *Zoom* magazine. At the checkout counter, she pokes through a jumble of key tags in a basket, and, selecting one with a large gold "M," she secures her new house keys.

"How are you, Madelyn?" someone says, making her jump. Pauline Redding at the cash register pushes her glasses up her nose with her index finger. "I'm real sorry about what happened. Frank and I have always felt so safe out in Willow Park. Now he's worried about me coming home after dark."

"I'm better, thanks." With a quick smile, she pockets change from $5 and retraces her steps to the street, her face aflame. Does everybody in the neighborhood know? She turns up her coat collar against the cold.

As she passes Goodman's Department Store, she glances at her image in the long expanse of glass. Before her surgery last March she would have assessed her posture or her hemline. Now her eyes rivet on the place where her breast used to be: Is the padding in place? Are the two sides even? Can anyone looking at her tell? She realizes with a start that it is not her own oval face that returns her gaze but the elongated, time-worn face of her mother, Rose McCandless.

As she lifts her hand to touch her cheek, the reflected buildings behind her blur, the traffic noises grow silent, and the face changes once again. Rose no longer returns her stare, nor the woman Madelyn Ives, but the twenty-two-year-old face of Maddy McCandless, a graduate student with short-cropped hair and a mouth that trembles with uncertainty.

She stands motionless in a stubbled field, facing the icy winter wind. In her hand is a shred of paper bearing words smudged by tears and melting snowflakes—words that would change her life.

If only she had known what lay ahead, thinks Madelyn Ives. "Never regret the things you've done," Grampa McCandless once told her, "only the things you haven't done." Good advice, but not always possible. For instance, if she had gone straight home last Friday instead of to a film . . . . That choice she'll regret for the rest of her life.

"Hey, lady," says a gravelly voice at her shoulder. She spins toward it, her dream state shattered by alarm. The man wipes his nose on the sleeve of his filthy overcoat and thrusts his grizzled chin within inches of her face. "Ya got a little somethin' for me?"

Madelyn grips her purse with both hands and backs away, nearly gagging on the panic that lodges in her throat. "No!" she croaks. "Get away!" She wills herself to run, but as in her nightmare her feet—leaden with fear—refuse to obey. *I'm going to die. This time he'll kill me.* She knows she should pay attention, do something in her own defense, but a women keeps crying "No, no, no!" and she can't think clearly. Pinpoints of light prickle behind her eyes as a force pressures the breath from her lungs and her head toward the pavement. But just as her knees turn to jelly, the cries stop, and she feels a strong hand grip her elbow to steady her.

"Move on, Dude," says a young man's voice. He holds her firmly upright until the flickering recedes, the heaviness abates, and the world rights itself again.

"Take it easy," he says, "Nobody's going to hurt you." He studies her face with concern for a moment, then slowly releases her. "You're not going to pass out on me, are you? You're okay now, right?"

With effort, Madelyn gathers herself. "Yes," she lies. "Thank you, I'm fine." She isn't fine. She isn't fine at all. She will never be fine again in this out-of-control world where madmen attack her in the dark, where creeps torment her with phone calls, where at any time the teredo can return to eat away another part of her body. She disengages her arm from his grasp and stoops to retrieve her parcel from the pavement, her discolored face flushed with embarrassment. Managing only a grimace for a smile, she edges away from the young man and hurries down Harding Boulevard.

At 14th Street she forces herself to slow her pace and take a deep, calming breath. "Control," she repeats like a mantra. "Get control."

All morning she has looked forward to treating Wynn to lunch at DiYanni's—both as a gesture of thanks and a show of strength. But the encounter with the vagrant has so unnerved her that she wishes only to run away, to board a Greyhound heading for Terre Haute or Topeka or Tucson—it doesn't matter where as long as it isn't Belleporte, Ohio.

Without Wynn's solid support and quirky humor, Madelyn doubts she could have gotten through Jessie's rebellious teens, the terror of cancer, or the erosion of her twenty-two-year marriage. Now she needs Wynn again—to make her laugh and to reassure her of her sanity.

By the time she reaches DiYanni's, she has regained her composure and is able to smile at Wynn, who signals her from a window table overlooking Buckeye Park.

With her dark glasses shoved atop her sun-streaked hair and her tanned, ringless hands folded in front of her, Wynn displays a serenity and confidence that Madelyn finds fortifying. She slips into the opposite chair and locks her hands in her lap to camouflage her trembling fingers.

"How'd you sleep?" asks Wynn. Receiving a shrug for an answer, she studies her friend closely. Even heavy makeup can't mask the tension that reveals itself in the tightening of Madelyn's jaw, the hide-and-seek dimple that has elongated into a weary crease at the corner of her smile. "Did you tell Steffan about the calls?"

"Yes. Have you decided what to order?"

As if on cue, a waiter sets a basket of rolls in front of them, hands Madelyn a menu, and disappears.

Throughout the meal, Madelyn half listens as Wynn talks about her nursery business: about the slipping gears on the second-hand backhoe she has purchased from Davis Brothers, about the landscaping contract she has signed with Belleporte General Hospital.

Madelyn envies her friend's autonomy as owner of Greenscape, which she built from scratch after her young firefighter husband lost his life beneath a collapsing roof. Hard work has never daunted Wynn, who lived for two years in a primitive shed while she was developing her twelve acres of healthy farmland, nurturing cuttings, and pruning other people's trees for gas and grocery money. Alone, she built arbors and fences, hauled gravel by the truckload, even glazed her first greenhouse with her own hands. Through it all, she had never lost her faith in herself, or her good humor.

"She cried when I left," says Wynn.

"Who cried?"

"Mother. In the nursing home. You haven't heard a

71

---

word I said." She pushes her empty plate aside. "Talk to me, Mad. What's going on in your head?"

Madelyn gazes out the window at a young mother in jeans pushing a stroller slowly through the park. The woman gazes dreamily at the bare treetops while her child, in a blue snowsuit, kicks its legs in delight.

"That was me twenty years ago," she says. Her eyes follow the stroller until it disappears into the trees. "I used to fit so comfortably into my life," she says. "But now I feel like a number eight foot in a size seven shoe."

Wynn smiles at the image. "You've had a tough year."

"I handled the teredo," says Madelyn. "Then Jessie left, and I handled that. Then David left, then Mother." She sips her coffee and sets the cup gently in its saucer. "I thought I was handling it all. But obviously not."

"What makes you say that?"

"Headaches," she says. "Homer Pritchard says I just need glasses, but I know it's not that simple. The pain comes in waves up my neck and across the back of my head to my temples." She demonstrates with her hands. "The kind that three Tylenol can't even touch."

"What else?"

"Truthfully, for the last two nights I've hardly slept at all. At 3 a.m. I'm up and pacing or watching *Bonanza*

72

reruns."

"And?"

"And I cry over the least little thing. Maybe David was right all along—I really do have a screw loose."

"I hardly think so."

"What *do* you think?"

"That last spring you underwent very scary major surgery, that your husband, daughter, and mother have abandoned you, that you're burned out at work, and that some low-life cretin has just violated you in the privacy of your own home. If that isn't enough to make anybody see double, cry, and watch *Bonanza*, I don't know what is!"

She signals the waiter. "Bring us two Black Jacks on the rocks."

"You left out a couple of things," says Madelyn, laughing in spite of herself.

"Tell me."

A white dog with a red neckerchief trots along the edge of the park, pausing at intervals to sniff and lift its leg. Suddenly it freezes in place, ears and tail erect, then lopes back the way it came.

"I see things," says Madelyn. "It's like I lose my grip on reality for a moment, drift off somewhere, re-run a tape in my mind of events that happened years ago."

"You're tired, Mad. Bone tired. Fatigue can make anybody punchy."

"Just now on the way over here I had a sort of seizure, a panic attack right on the street. It was awful."

Wynn takes her hand, gripping hard to control its trembling. "Believe me, I know about panic attacks. When Sam died, I went crazy, hurling dishes against the wall. How dare the world go on as if nothing of significance had been lost? For six months I awakened in the middle of the night in a cold sweat, panting, my pulse rate off the charts, convinced I was about to die."

"You never told me."

"What would have been the point? You couldn't bring Sam back." She shakes her head, remembering. "No one could help me. Only time—and hard work."

"Well, you certainly did a lot of that."

The waiter makes a small ceremony of setting two short glasses before them. Then he withdraws.

Madelyn so seldom sees Wynn without a straw hat and sunglasses that she sometimes forgets the unusual blue of her eyes, the streak of gray sweeping back from her forehead. Her heart swells with love for this friend whose quiet strength restores her equilibrium. "I know a bit about loss," she says. "I don't think I've ever told you about Adam Devlin."

"Tell me now."

Madelyn sips her bourbon, feeling its warmth slide

74

to her stomach. "I was at Ohio State finishing my master's," she says. "David had graduated and was working in his dad's insurance business to earn enough money for graduate school. We planned to marry in June."

She splays her fingers, studying her wedding band. "I shared a small apartment with Marisol Baya, who ate only vegetables, and spoke staccato Spanish when she was excited, which was most of the time. Her friends argued about Mao and drank ouzo and listened to sitar music— totally unlike my friends, who pursued law and medicine and liked to debate politics over a $6 jug of Chianti."

Madelyn traces the rim of her glass with her finger, her face flushed with remembrance. "One night I came in late from a seminar to find our living room jammed with artists and musicians. At Mari's insistence, I sat on a kitchen stool and listened while one member of the group read aloud to the others. He stood in the center of the room, holding his book like a choir boy, and read from *Letters to Imlay* by Mary Wollstonecraft, the subject of my nearly completed master's thesis. Like the others, I sat enchanted, listening to his lyrical voice. Only afterwards, as we talked in the kitchen over pizza, did I notice his stained fingernails and ragged jeans."

"An artist?" asks Wynn.

"A wood carver, majoring in economics. There was something in his look—a directness, a sort of frank assessment of my intelligence, my worth as a person." She smiles crookedly. "No one has, before or since, looked at me in quite that way."

"Did he intend to make a living as a wood carver?"

For a long moment Madelyn sits motionless, her gaze unfocused. "I never knew what he meant to do with his art," she says. "He gave me the impression that he didn't plan to pursue it professionally—just to purge it from his system before he got serious about his life."

"So then?"

Madelyn sets her glass on its paper coaster. "I fell in love—not just with Adam but also with his friends who lived in a sort of artists' commune, a rustic place with no phone, no hot water. But Falter Farm did have rolling fields, a creek, and a large stand of hardwoods." She smiles, remembering. "Adam had a pet raccoon named Dub, short for Double-oh-Seven because of the rings around his eyes."

"Were you lovers?" asks Wynn, her voice soft as snowfall.

"Yes, but only once. Adam knew about David, that we were committed."

"Go on."

Madelyn lifts her shoulders and sighs. "One afternoon near the end of the semester, I drove out to the farm and found a scribbled note taped to the barn door: Adam's father had had a heart attack. He was going home to Florida and would call when he knew his plans. But he didn't call, and he didn't return to school. Someone shipped his belongings to Gainesville.

"After a couple of weeks, I tried to contact him, but the number he had provided was out of service. He had closed his father's house and gone elsewhere. I didn't know how to find him."

"And he never contacted you, not even a letter?"

She shook her head. "Nothing. For over a month, I made excuses. He had a lot on his mind—arranging for the funeral, selling the house. By that time it was May, and graduation was just around the corner. David kept calling me, urging me to make wedding plans."

"Did you ever find out what happened?"

"Never," says Madelyn, avoiding Wynn's eyes. "A few years ago I tried to find him online, but I came up empty." Her mouth hardened. "I regarded it as the cruelest betrayal of friendship." She feels her throat tightening, the tears pressing against the backs of her eyes. "Two months later, David and I married at his parents' home in Chagrin Falls. End of story."

She is grateful when the waiter approaches, his pencil poised. "Dessert, ladies?"

"Just the check," she manages to say.

77

Silence stretches between them when he leaves. Madelyn rotates the salt shaker and stares unseeing at the bare limbs of a buckeye tree in the park. "Next to you, I feel like such a wimp," she says.

"Don't be absurd," says Wynn. "Have you called that woman from STAAR who talked with you in the hospital?"

Madelyn shakes her head. "Part of me says I should. But another part feels I need to handle this on my own—to feel competent, able—not dependent upon David or you or some support group. It's a choice of either taking charge of the situation or being victimized by it."

Suddenly she brightens. "I forgot to tell you the *good* news. As of yesterday I'm officially on leave of absence until summer. I told Friedman I need time to 'finish my photo essay.'" She grins wickedly. "What I didn't tell him was that I also need time to start it."

Wynn laughs. "That's great, Mad. You've talked about this for years."

Madelyn sobers. "The trouble is, I need a place to work." She pulls cash from an envelope and places it on top of the check. "What I really need to do is get out of this town," she says. "Go someplace where I can sleep and heal and get control of my life."

Wynn thinks for a moment, then leans forward on

her elbows and looks hard into her friend's face. "How do you feel about cats?"

"Cats?"

"And neighbors who don't knock?"

"What kind of question is that?"

"It's the perfect solution," says Wynn with an abracadabra sweep of her hands. "You need a place to hibernate. I need someone to take care of Boots and oversee Mother's house until I can decide what to do with it. It's far from fancy, hardly more than a cottage, but it's right on one of the most beautiful beaches in Florida. What do you think?"

"I think," says Madelyn, "that you're an angel delivering a gift from the gods."

Chapter 9
Tuesday, December 16

By five o'clock that same afternoon Madelyn has packed two suitcases and left a message at police headquarters for Sergeant Steffan, telling him that he can reach her at Wynn's for the next day or two. As she stands near the front window, watching for the yellow cab that will deliver her to Greenscape, her eyes sweep back and forth across the front lawn, seeing neither the male cardinal on the bird feeder nor the scarlet poinsettia still visible in the gathering dusk. Instead she concentrates on the oak tree that had concealed the man in the ski mask. What if he's out there now? she thinks, stepping back from the window. She presses her fingers into her aching stomach and wishes she could shake the feeling of being watched. Had something moved just there near the woodpile?

She half turns at the sound of the telephone and waits, rigid with tension, while the machine records the call. As usual, the line remains open even though no one leaves a message after the beep. Please, please let us get him this time, she thinks.

Not having a car makes her feel frantic, a sitting duck. At Wynn's she'll feel less threatened, but she'll still be stuck without transportation as all three of Greenscape's trucks are in constant use. How will she pass the time until the Belleporte police proclaim it's safe to return to Willow Park? On sudden impulse she grabs the Yellow Pages and circles the number for Erie AutoServe under "Automobiles—Rental."

Forty-five minutes later she stuffs her receipt and drivers' license into her purse and accepts the keys to her newly rented Ford Escort.

As the counter clerk loads her luggage into the back, Madelyn adjusts the mirrors and fastens her seatbelt, feeling decisive, competent. One problem solved. She savors a small twinge of pleasure knowing how David would regard her choice of cars. *Jesus, Madelyn, don't you know all sub-compact cars are deathmobiles?*

She locates the headlight switch, then backs the Ford out of the lot, glad to be rid of the clerk's skeptical stares at her discolored eye and sutured earlobe. If she's careful not to make any sudden movements, she finds she can maneuver with her right arm, sparing her painful rib. The clock on the dash agrees with her wristwatch: 6:17 p.m.

Uneasy driving a strange car, especially on a rainy road surface, she heads south on Butler Road toward farm country, turning on the radio for company. Avalanches in Colorado. Mudslides in California. A Columbian plane has exploded, killing 153. Until recently, she listened with detachment to such reports. Belleporte is, after all, a long way from Bogota. But four nights ago her comfort, her confidence, and her sense of security were stripped away in ten horror-filled minutes. She slams her hand on the steering wheel in renewed outrage.

Slowing to read a road sign, Madelyn wishes Wynn's house weren't so remote. Beyond her headlights stretch miles of empty blacktop flanked by deep ditches. At least the rain hasn't yet turned to snow. She switches on the windshield wipers and forces herself to think happier thoughts. Like enrolling in the advanced photography course being offered in January at the Cleveland Museum of Art.

Telling Wynn about Adam has stirred a longing in her that she hasn't felt in years—a yearning for her younger self, whose life stretched before her in a wide, bright ribbon

83

of possibility. If nothing else, the intervening years have taught her how tenuous health and happiness can be. Better to grab them while they last, while the teredo lies dormant and the rapist is at bay.

When headlights appear in her rear view mirror, Madelyn automatically checks her speedometer and eases back on the accelerator. The last thing she needs is a speeding ticket and embarrassing scrutiny by the Lorain County police. But the headlights settle in behind her, apparently comfortable with her 45 m.p.h.

Although living alone is not her preference, she had begun to adjust to long evenings spent in her own company. Until last Friday, she had hit the floor running every morning, not stopping until 4 p.m.—lectures, student conferences, meetings—with little time to think, plan, draw a breath. After such a day, the thought of her study at home with its plush chair and good reading light welcomed like a homing beacon, its colors her colors—dark green and straw, with here and there a touch of burgundy.

She had savored the fragrances of her house, of lemon furniture polish and, in the summer, moist grass. She had looked forward to slipping into her old blue robe and enjoying a grilled cheese sandwich in front of the TV with her bare feet propped on the coffee table. But from now on, the home that she and David worked so hard to own and improve will forever harbor the stench of terror like some unlit alley in a barrio. Sorrow lumps up in her throat.

She misses David—not only for the security of another person's ears and eyes, but also for the lingering scent of his cologne in the steamy bathroom, the Sunday morning clutter of the *New York Times*, the steady rise and ebb of his breathing in the dark.

She turns right on Black Creek Road, noting with a flutter of concern that the car behind her does the same. She can tell by the height of the headlights that it's a truck or a van, therefore probably not the county vehicle she at first suspected. She checks her door locks, then tunes the radio to a classical music station, determined not to let anxiety take control.

Her thoughts return to the twenty-two-year history she and David share—a storehouse of mortgage payments, Thanksgiving turkeys, ballet lessons, and birthday parties.

Together they own chicken pox, a dead Black Labrador Retriever named Saxon, two smashed Oldsmobiles, a fractured tibia, a flooded basement, three funerals, a cancelled trip to China, and recently—a "post-nuptial agreement." The breast cancer is hers alone.

And now, rape.

Why do you always try to fix my life? Can't you just listen to my problems, just hear me out without offering any advice?

For Christ's sake, Madelyn, what's the point of telling me if you don't want me to respond?

At first, when David still adored her, he would brush her long hair while she regaled him with an embellished account of her day.

"One hopes," she would clown, lengthening her upper lip in exaggerated imitation of Dean Woolsy Hammet (called "Woolly Mammoth" behind his back) "that the integrity of Harding College will not be compromised by your position."

"Compromising your position is exactly what I have in mind," David would say as he swooped her up and carted her off to bed.

How long has it been since she welcomed David's caressing fingers, enjoyed the slick sweat of sex? A year? Nine months, at least. Not since the invasion of the teredo.

Left behind in her lingerie drawer is the sheer embroidered nightgown—David's homecoming gift after her surgery. Part of her hates him for his insensitivity, for the mockery it makes of her damaged body.

Madelyn lifts her eyes to the rearview mirror, startled to see the truck behind her pulling forward, close on her tail. Thank goodness, he's going to pass. She adjusts the rearview mirror for anti-glare and slows slightly to encourage the move. But to her surprise the driver also reduces speed, dropping back two car lengths. Maybe he's drunk, she thinks, glad that Wynn's turn-off is only another half-mile ahead.

She can tell the temperature is dropping from the patchy slick developing on the road surface. In the clearing sky a slender moon appears. It reminds Madelyn of a summer early in her marriage when she and David rented a log cabin at Little Bass Lake in Michigan, where they skinny dipped by moonlight and made love on gritty sheets. One day, they promised each other, they would buy the old Gardner cottage for their summer getaway. But it never happened.

For one thing Jessica, who burst into the world red-faced and screaming, continued her protest through every stage of childhood, leaving Madelyn drained of energy. Because Jessie's perversity heightened with every disruption of her routine, it seemed best, while she was little, not to uproot her.

Also, through David's careful planning, they directed their combined income toward paying off student loans and purchasing the house in Willow Park. By the time his future with Kohl and Sumner was secure, he had come to prefer a life of frequent traveling, feeling itchy when confined to Ohio for more than a month or two at a time. Eventually, the Gardners sold their cottage to newlyweds from Akron.

The lights following Madelyn suddenly extinguish, and she nearly swerves off the road while straining to see in the dark mirror. Had the truck stopped? A moment later she feels a bump from behind, and her grip tightens on the wheel, her heart in her throat. What the hell does he think he's doing?

Shaking with fright, she speeds up as much as she dares on the icy pavement, trying to put as much distance as she can between them. But once again, her Ford is hit from behind, this time with force on the left rear fender, and she winces in pain fighting to keep from sluing onto the gravel shoulder. She is crying now, fully aware of the driver's intent. He's trying to kill me. He wants to force me into the ditch. Her hand gropes for her cell phone, then remembers it was missing from her stolen purse.

She gasps in horror as a glint of moonlight reveals the truck bearing down on her for the third time. Frantically, she looks to the left and right, hoping for lights, a driveway, a farm house where she might find refuge.

This time when the crash comes, she hears the rip of metal, the shattering of glass. As if in a nightmare, she feels the Ford hurtle forward, spinning out of control. This is it, says a voice in her head. This is the way it all ends. With a scream lodged in her throat, she braces for the impact.

But it never comes. When the spinning stops,

Madelyn is dumfounded to find her right foot still jammed against the brake pedal, the engine still running, and the Ford parked neatly on the side of Black Creek Road facing the direction she wants to go. Fifty yards ahead is the sign marking the entrance to Greenscape, and just beyond are lights from Wynn's farmhouse. Her first impulse is to get out and run, but she forces herself to stay inside the locked car and get it moving as fast as she can.

She steps hard on the accelerator, causing the car to lurch forward with a terrible screech as the rear fender presses against the tire. Even with both hands gripping the steering wheel, Madelyn can barely keep the little Ford from wobbling and shuddering off into the ditch. Like a drunken ox, the car bucks and falters toward Greenscape, its driver hanging on with her last ounce of strength. As she rounds the corner into Wynn's driveway, she leans on the horn—a long blast that brings her friend hurrying from the house.

"What's happened?" Wynn cries as she sees Madelyn struggling from the damaged car. But Madelyn cannot speak. Wild-eyed with shock, she grasps Wynn's arm and together they stumble toward the open kitchen door.

An hour later, County Officer Brosky caps his pen and runs his fingers through his thinning hair. "By the way," he says, "it wasn't a truck that hit you. It was a van with local plates. Lots of damage to the front fender." He shakes his head. "Driver wasn't as lucky as you. Put himself nose first into the ditch, then took off on foot. We'll haul the vehicle in and look her over good. If we're lucky, she'll give us fingerprints or some other evidence that will identify him. In the meantime, call me if you have any further trouble. Number's at the top." He hands her a copy of the police report and replaces his hat. "Gonna be a cold one," he says turning up his collar. Wynn and Madelyn watch him negotiate the turnabout and vanish into the night.

Madelyn has just awakened when Neil Steffan calls at precisely 9 a.m. His voice is businesslike, his tone brusque. "Two new developments," he announces. "Number one, I just checked with Ohio Bell, and it looks like your breather is being careful to use a variety of phones." Madelyn's spirits plummet. "Number two, it was your own van that hit you. We checked the registration."

She grips the receiver, struggling to understand. "You mean the same bastard who raped me tried to kill me with my own car?"

"That's how it looks," he says. "Only he outfoxed himself and totaled the van instead."

"Good!" yells Madelyn, enraged. "I hope he killed himself."

Her outburst causes Steffan to choose his next words carefully. "You were wise to vacate when you did," he says. "If it was the same guy, the only way he could have been behind you on that country road was if he'd been watching you and followed your cab to the car rental." He clears his throat. "Got to be someone who knows the neighborhood," he says half to himself. "Someone familiar with the house and grounds."

"Well, he can have 'em," Madelyn says, fury ringing in her voice. "And good riddance! I'm getting the hell out of this town today—even if I have to charter a plane!"

Chapter 10
Wednesday, December 17

Glancing about to be sure he is alone, he sets aside the shovel and pulls the small jeweler's box from his pocket. With callused fingers, he removes the lid and lifts the square of cotton inside. No more gold necklace, thanks to Rollo—only a single diamond earring.

Close. He had come so close. If he shuts his eyes, he can almost feel her body beneath him, almost smell her flowery hair. He thrills, remembering her blood on his knife blade, the perfume of fear and flowers.

Too bad about the wheels. Lost traction on the ice and wham, right into the fucking ditch. Got out of there just in time. At least Rollo had sold the cell phone and the necklace for cash—although not for as much as he'd hoped.

He zips the box into his inside pocket, then picks up the spade again, feeling the heat in his groin, the anger tightening his chest.

     With each vicious stabbing of the earth, he widens and deepens the hole, humming to himself to drown out the whine of the locusts in his head.

     Soon, he promises her. Real soon.

Chapter 11
Wednesday, December 17

❝How far is it?" Madelyn asks the cab driver. His picture, featuring greasy hair and a drooping black moustache, glowers at her from the license pinned to the back of his headrest. She decides Arnold Capo looks like a B-movie thug from Central Casting. She pushes aside thoughts of last evening's terrifying trip to Wynn's house and forces herself not to check behind for a tailgater.

"About 60 miles," he says. "We stay on Waldo Road, which is route 24, almost all the way to the coast. At the last minute, we cut over to 326." He checks his watch. "Should be on Cypress Key before sundown."

As the strip malls and clutter of outer Gainesville give way to countryside, Madelyn settles back against the plastic seat and savors a rush of anticipation. Just sand and sunshine—no jarring telephone calls, no worrisome hate mail, no final exams to grade. Even if this place turns out to be a tacky, overpriced tourist haven, she'll always be grateful to Wynn for providing refuge, both here and in Belleporte, when she needed it most. She closes her eyes, vowing to let nothing spoil the next few weeks.

Her first response, when Wynn had offered her mother's cottage, was eager acceptance, but after their lunch at DiYanni's, she began to compile a mental list of all the reasons she couldn't leave Belleporte: How on earth would she inform Jessica where to call in case of emergency? And who would meet Rose's plane at the end of her Caribbean cruise? Who would shovel the driveway if it snowed? And suppose David should want—what? To come home for Christmas? To fly to Mexico for a quickie divorce?

Typically, Wynn neutralized each irrational concern with a healthy dose of logic. She would, she promised, gladly serve as shoveler, chauffeur, and amanuensis. With Ohio Bell and Sergeant Steffan keeping daily tabs on Madelyn's telephone calls, all family messages would be received and forwarded. "Get dressed," she had ordered. "I've just booked you on a 12:55 Delta flight to Gainesville. We're leaving for the airport in 45 minutes." Then she had grinned, pleased with herself. "You owe me one."

Madelyn hugged her. "More than one, I'm afraid. I just wish you were coming with me."

"And look at you every morning in that loathsome rag of a bathrobe? Thanks but no thanks."

Now here she is, five hours later, crossing the Seminole Causeway and Bridge connecting Cypress Key to Gulf Coast Florida.

Arnold Capo rolls down the window and points out to sea. "Out there's Turncoat Key where the loggerheads lay their eggs every spring." He shifts his gum from port to starboard. "Quite a sight, those big old turtles digging them deep nests up above the tide line and dropping in a couple hundred eggs at a time. Loggerheads are endangered, you know. Folks around here are real protective. Next island over is Owl Key—ain't nobody lived there since a hurricane wiped out the whole village more'n a hundred years ago. That's Cypress Key dead ahead."

Below them, the Gulf of Mexico glitters golden in the late afternoon sunlight; white gulls follow in the wake of a shrimp boat heading to harbor.

Madelyn's throat constricts. She remembers clutching David's hand as the company plane approached the runway at San Juan fifteen years ago. Just the two of them, running away to Puerto Rico in the middle of an Ohio blizzard, leaving her mother Rose to cope with Jessica's tantrums. How happy they had been in that long

97

ago December, how accepting of their imperfect lives.

Islands have always enchanted Madelyn—as if crossing over water automatically breaches some invisible barrier and thrusts one into a whole new persona for whom all things are possible. On this island, she thinks, I can be anyone I choose.

While Arnold stops at the Visitors' Center for directions, she waits in the cab making a list: groceries, post cards, stamps, sunscreen. And a wide-brimmed straw hat. She taps the pencil on her lip. Maybe she'll splurge and get some prescription sun glasses. Homer Pritchard must be right after all about the source of her headaches. She used her new reading glasses during the whole flight without a hint of pain.

"South end," says Arnold, handing her a map through the window. "All the way to the end of the strand where it turns into Beacon Point Road."

Shaped roughly like a backwards "C," the island curls around an inner harbor where fishing boats bob in their slips, naturally protected from the incoming gulf surge. Madelyn is charmed by the town that includes a few stores, an old frame hotel, a post office, and a combination library and local history museum.

They follow Harbor Road south along the edge of Lake May past Papa Pelican's, the Crow's Nest, and a string of boutiques and trinket shops peddling T-shirts and shell jewelry. The cab heads east on Beacon Point Road, then northeast toward the marshes, finally stopping before a small, weathered house, standing aloof from its neighbors on a slight rise above the gulf.

"This here's got to be number 123—Hayes Cottage. You got a key?" Arnold pulls into a turnabout at the rear of the house and hauls Madelyn's tripod and two suitcases from the trunk. Breathing heavily, he carries them up three wooden steps to the deck that extends along the right side and across the front facing the beach. He wipes his brow with his handkerchief and steps forward, taking in the long stretch of white sand. "Nice," he says. "Real nice."

Madelyn digs in her purse for her wallet and the envelope containing house keys and emergency numbers.

"I'll manage from here," she says, handing him the fare and a generous tip. "Many thanks."

He nods and retreats, leaving her alone to savor the salt breeze redolent of seaweed and the heady tang of independence.

"Bless you, Wynn," she whispers.

To her surprise, the refrigerator contains an unopened quart of skim milk, a small tub of margarine, a six-pack of Michelob, a package of English muffins, and a glass casserole covered with aluminum foil. She lifts one corner and sniffs with pleasure: chicken and wild rice. Her stomach growls.

Part of her wants to explore each cupboard, investigate every closet, poke into the medicine cabinet, the pantry, the old seaman's chest in the corner of the kitchen. She wants to read all the titles in the bookcases on either side of the stone fireplace, test the mattresses in the upstairs and downstairs bedrooms, pump up the tires of the old Schwinn in the carport and go for a ride. But another part wants to take it slowly, to prolong the pleasure and savor each discovery.

"Open your birthday gifts, dear. Your guests are waiting."

"I will, Mama. After awhile"

"That's not polite, Madelyn. You need to open them while the children are here so you can say a proper thank you."

"All of them?"

"Yes, all."

"Can't I save just one for later?"

"Don't be willful, Madelyn. Open the presents."

She has, she reminds herself, several weeks of self-indulgence ahead of her, so she might as well start by easing into idle mode. Pulling off her shoes and her pantyhose, she leaves them where they fall. She washes her face free of make-up and shrugs into jeans and Jessie's oversized blue sweatshirt. Then with her camera slung over her shoulder, she follows a short, wooden boardwalk to the beach.

In just ten minutes the daylight has changed, and the air has cooled. Gilt-edged clouds have temporarily imprisoned the sun, which fans protesting rays in all directions. Madelyn walks at the edge of the surf where the moist sand gives beneath her feet. Sea water oozes into each footprint she leaves behind, softening the edges and smoothing over the traces of human intrusion. Just like Hansel and Gretel's bread crumbs, she thinks—gone before they could lead the children home.

A black lab puppy, its shiny coat glistening with sea water, lopes to Madelyn's side and drops a stick at her feet. It sits abruptly, tongue lolling, poised to spring at her first response. He looks a bit like Jessie's dog, Pepper, whose sweet nature endured despite the child's rough, sometimes cruel treatment. Poor Pepper had died beneath the wheels of a school bus. Together she and Jessica had buried her behind the garage alongside a gerbil and several goldfish.

"I'll play your silly game," Madelyn says to the pup. She tosses the stick into the surf, aware of a surging happiness—for the lighthouse in silhouette out on the point and for the red sun dancing on the rim of the horizon.

"Hello-o-o." Madelyn jerks awake, suddenly paralyzed with fear. Someone is downstairs. Her eyes dart around the unfamiliar room, seeking a weapon, a place to hide.

"Yo, Madelyn. You up?"

A woman's voice. She knows my name. And coffee. I smell coffee. Madelyn's fear ebbs as she recalls the neighbor Wynn told her about, the one who never knocks.

Inhaling deeply to calm her nerves, she pulls on her robe over her "I ♥ BCO" T-shirt, runs her fingers through her feathery curls, and descends to the kitchen.

"Bad timing," says a tall woman, handing her a mug of coffee. "It's my trademark," She wears painter's overalls and thong sandals. Shooing a large black and white cat off the kitchen table, she sets a plate of steaming muffins in the center. "I'm Orbison from next door, and this is the only thing I know how to cook—bran muffins, guaranteed to make you shit for a week. I see from the look on your face that Wynn didn't warn you."

Madelyn laughs. "As a matter of fact, she did." She squints at the ceiling and affects Wynn's drawl. "Don't mind Felene Orbison. She plays by her own rules." She breaks a muffin in two and takes a bite. "Ummm, yum. And that creature, I take it, is Boots."

"Definitely low maintenance," says Felene. "Just keep him in kibbles. He comes and goes at will." She scratches the cat under the chin. "Well anyway, I've got errands to run this morning and thought you might like to tag along, see the island, pick up a few supplies." She tucks a strand of salt-and-pepper hair behind one ear.

"Sounds good," says Madelyn. She has already decided she likes this woman whose stern, lined face can't quite mask the twinkle in her eye. "Is there a bookstore?

"Two, neither of them worth a damn. But you can order what you want." She refills her cup. "Do you windsurf?"

Inwardly, Madelyn recoils, thinking swim suit, scars, questions. "I'm not much into sports, I'm afraid. Do you?"

"Every morning. Great fun. Keeps the gut in shape. What's this BCO you love?"

Madelyn looks down at the gap in her robe. "Belleporte Community Orchestra. And I don't, really. They're terrible. But I'm a sucker for supporting the arts."

Her companion cocks her head and smiles for the first time. "Call me Fee," she says, standing. "I'll honk in thirty minutes."

Fee's old Volvo has neither shock absorbers nor air-conditioning, so Madelyn rolls down the window and hangs on tightly with both hands as they bounce and lurch along rutted back roads. She breathes in the fragrant salt marshes, their brown and golden grasses nodding toward the gulf in the offshore breeze. A turkey buzzard levitates at their approach and wheels out of sight. Fee turns onto a gravel road and heads north toward the village.

A moment later she swings into a rutted driveway and winds back through the trees. "Perfect," she says, glancing at her watch. "Bread's just coming out of the oven."

Chickens scatter as she parks in a cluttered yard and honks once. Immediately a brown raisin of a woman emerges from an old frame shack, clasping herself tightly with both arms. She wears a blood-stained apron that reaches the tops of her feet.

"Morning, Minneola. How's the hip?"

"Doin' better, Miss Fee. Buckweed poultice put her right again." Her ancient face splits in a grin. "What you want today?"

Fee beckons to Madelyn, and together they follow the old woman into the house. "The usual," she says, "except twice over. This is Madelyn Ives, Wynn's friend. She's staying at Hayes Cottage. Madelyn, meet Minneola Jones—witch, faith healer, and the best bread baker this side of Paris, France."

"Ooo, chile, you got the look," says Minneola, shaking her head. "You shore got the look." She stands on tiptoe and squints upward into Madelyn's face. "Yes'm, Minneola got her work cut out, for dang sure."

"What sort of look is that?" asks Madelyn with a smile. But Minneola goes about her business, wrapping two fragrant loaves in paper towels, humming tunelessly under her breath.

When she has stowed the still warm bread in Fee's canvas carryall, the old woman hobbles into her pantry, pulling the door closed behind her. Fee winks at Madelyn and holds her finger to her lips. A moment later Minneola reappears carrying a tightly covered jar full of greenish paste. With great care, she spoons two small mounds of the stuff onto a square of waxed paper, which she folds into a bundle and wraps tightly with string.

"Make into four," says Minneola, handing the parcel to Madelyn. "Two with your night meal, two on Thursday. You come see Minneola at gibbous." She nods to Fee, who hands her $5.

As they drive off, Madelyn explodes in laughter. "Surely she doesn't expect me to eat that stuff! And what in hell is 'gibbous'?"

"It means she wants you to come back on the twenty-sixth when there's a three-quarter moon."

Madelyn glances at her new friend in surprise. "You

SUSAN B. JOHNSON

believe this stuff?"

Fee smiles indulgently, her eyes on the road ahead. "Minneola knows things about people," she says. "For instance, two years ago I had to have my tonsils removed, and my throat hurt so much I couldn't eat for a week. No amount of pleading would persuade Doc Percy to give me anything stronger than Tylenol." She smiles, remembering. "But Minneola understood my agony. She cooked up this gummy sort of root concoction and told me to chew. At first it hurt like hell, but an hour later, most of the pain was gone."

"What was it?"

"Doesn't matter what it was, only that it worked. Six months later I read an article that explained why." Fee parks in front of Larry's IGA and rolls up her window. "Seems the muscles around such a wound lock into a kind of suspended animation to protect against further strain or infection. By chewing Minneola's homemade gum, I stimulated them and got them working again."

"How could she know that?"

Fee shrugs. "Same way she knows the exact moment to plant pumpkins or whether Eva Jasper's third child will be another boy. Minneola just knows."

"What do you suppose she meant about 'having the look'?"

"Hard to say. Could mean she sees sickness coming on, or maybe she senses you're under some kind of emotional strain." She shifts in her seat to face Madelyn. "Folks around here respect Minneola's 'knowings,' as she calls them. Islanders are quick to share success stories about her potions and predictions—unless, of course, they sense you're a doubter." Fee unclasps her seatbelt and reaches for the door handle. "I know damn near every person on this island, and I've never heard a one of them call Minneola wrong. If I were you, I'd do exactly as she says."

Chapter 12
Saturday, December 20

Having left Ohio in a rush, Madelyn's two suitcases had seriously limited her present wardrobe. So she spends Saturday morning buying clothes—including a lightweight pair of slacks, a white cotton sweater, and a long denim skirt that she couldn't resist. For the next couple of hours she selects Christmas gifts from a cluster of stores along the strand, settling on a lavender mohair shawl for her mother and another gold chain for Jess. From Barbara's Book Nook she buys *Cooking With Homegrown Herbs* for Wynn and for herself *The Place of No Roads* by photographer Ville Lenkkeri. And just in case it turns out that "the arrangement" with David includes a holiday gift exchange, she is ready with all four volumes of *The Alexandrian Quartet* by Lawrence Durrell, his favorite author. She smiles to herself when she adds up what she has spent—over $800. Time to loosen up.

After lunching on shrimp salad at Papa Pelican's, she stuffs her sandals into one of her shopping bags and walks home along the beach, making mental photographs of driftwood and sand dollars and the old lighthouse out on the point. Nothing can diminish the pleasure she takes in this worry-free afternoon, not even this morning's unsettling telephone conversation with Neil Steffan.

"Your breather has quit the game," he had said. "Not one call since you left."

"That's good, right?"

"Probably."

"Why only probably?"

"Well, it could mean—"

"For God's sake, what?"

"It could mean that somehow he knows you've left town." He tapped his fingernails impatiently against the receiver.

"Well, even if he does, he has no idea where I've gone. Nobody knows except you and Gil Everhart and my friend Wynn Skyler, who loaned me this house."

"Are you positive nobody else knows?"

"I'm sure."

"Good. Let's keep it that way." His voice revealed a

new tone, distracted and remote, as if he had more pressing business elsewhere. "Phone company's terminated their audit," he says, "but we're keeping an eye on the house just in case. By the way, your pal Manolo no longer works for Tune 'n Lube. Apparently his boss caught him smoking dope on the job and fired him."

Inwardly, she shudders. "I'm just glad I'm here and he's not."

"Yeah, well we can't find him. Any, any idea where he might have gone? We'd sure like to talk to him." But she hadn't known what to suggest.

Madelyn walks along the edge of the surf, determined to enjoy the cool salt water on the tops of her sunburned feet. She did the right thing by breaking it off with Vic. The longer she allowed the flirtation to continue, the harder it would be to disengage down the line. She realizes that until now she hasn't thought of him once since leaving Ohio. Coming to this lovely place has lifted her spirits and helped put the fear behind her. For the last three nights she has slept dreamlessly for at least nine hours.

Yet as much as she is enjoying Hayes Cottage, the rapist still lurks behind her scrim of happiness. The ring of the telephone or a stranger at her door still shatters her peace of mind and rattles her nerves.

Boots rouses himself from the door mat and follows her into the kitchen, anticipating the joy of empty shopping bags. Madelyn scoops him up and hugs him. "You lucky old reprobate! What a self-indulgent life you lead!"

When she opens the refrigerator for the pitcher of ice tea, she finds an invitation from Fee thumb-tacked to a grapefruit wearing a black felt-tipped frown. "Deliver me from cocktail parties," it says. "Wash your feet and come on over about seven-thirty."

At six she showers, then slips into her new petal pink velour robe of which she is certain Wynn will approve. She applies gloss and lotion to her sunburned lips and cheeks, then steps back to measure the effect. Not bad, she thinks. Mouth a bit wide. A new crop of freckles. She touches her ear lobe, stitches out and nearly healed, and pulls closed the robe's lapels to conceal her scars.

Down on the floor, bitch! Will that voice never stop?

Across the bed fans her new white silk dress, an indulgence for which she offers no apologies. She glances at the bedside clock, then perches on the dormer seat with Boots in her lap and peeks through the shutter.

A hundred yards down the beach she can see Fee's house, an amorphous structure of weathered cypress rambling willy-nilly across a small dune. Several cars already occupy the drive.

Like the wives of doctors and diplomats, Madelyn has grown accustomed to making social appearances without escort. Until recently, she has enjoyed the latitude it affords her—to arrive and leave when she chooses and to mingle with those whom she finds interesting rather than with those who are good for business. But since her "arrangement" with David, she has begun to miss an intimacy they have rarely shared in the past ten years. She yearns for an arm to hold and the reassuring sense of couplehood.

The walls of Anna Hayes' bedroom have flowered wallpaper and rose-painted wainscoting proclaiming feminine occupancy. *Some women—like Wynn and her mother—live whole lives without men,* Madelyn reminds herself. Thrilled and frightened by the prospect, she shifts Boots to a cushion and bends forward to brush her hair.

Luminarias line the steps to Fee's gulfside deck, where the party is in full swing. Madelyn pauses to brush the sand from her bare feet and to slip into her high-heeled sandals; then drawing a deep breath, she climbs toward the music of a lute or perhaps a classical guitar.

"Jo Patton," says a pretty woman, holding out her hand. "Fee asked me to watch for you. Madelyn Ives, right?"

"Right," says Madelyn with a smile. She is as grateful for Jo's green silk chemise as for the friendly greeting, putting to rest her concern that she might be

SUSAN B. JOHNSON

overdressed.

"Let's get you a glass of wine. Follow me."

They cross the lantern-lit deck to the French doors opening into the interior, where Madelyn stops, stunned by the unexpected. A cathedral ceiling looms over the spacious living room appointed entirely in black and white—white carpeting, black walls, white drapes, black leather sofa and chairs, a white orchid in a black onyx vase. The wall opposite the deck is dominated by three enormous, black-and-white photographs. She studies the curve of a nude waist and hip in repose, a Nodding Tern on its nest of eggs, and the lined face of an old woman upturned to the sun,. The effect is so elegant, so serene, so un-Fee-like that for a moment Madelyn forgets to breathe.

Fee herself wears a floor-length scarlet kimono. The ivory chopsticks spiking from her iron-gray chignon match her wide carved bracelet. Across the room she catches Madelyn's eye and lifts her chin in salute.

"So, this is your first visit to Cypress Key?" asks Jo, handing Madelyn a wine glass with a slender stem.

"Yes. I'm on sabbatical from the college where I teach. My friend Wynn Skyler—do you know Wynn?"

"Of course," says her companion. "Everybody knows everybody here. It's both a blessing and a curse." Jo's throaty laugh draws the attention of a couple standing

114

nearby. "Madelyn Ives, meet Allison and Kent Jacoby, who own and operate the Harbor Inn, that old hotel down on First."

"Oh, it's wonderful," says Madelyn. "I saw it the other day when Fee showed me around the island. She says you have a terrific kitchen."

"Terrific chef," corrects Kent. "Terrible kitchen." His grin creeps up his left cheek. "But we're working on it."

Allison slips her arm around his waist. "The place had been boarded up for twelve years when we bought it four years ago. Since then we've made major repairs—new plumbing, wiring, roof. Redoing the kitchen is the last big project." She helps herself from a tray of hors d'oeuvres offered by a waiter in black uniform. "Stop by someday. I'll show you around. If you're lucky, you might encounter Miss Lily."

Madelyn cocks her head. "And she is—?"

"Our resident ghost," laughs Kent. "In 1877 a young woman named Lily Eastman hurled herself from the upper balcony. Her remains are buried in Three Oaks Cemetery, but her restless spirit is said to roam the upper halls." He bugs his eyes and flutters his fingers.

Madelyn grins. "I'd love to do a photo study of your inn while I'm here. What's a good day?"

Allison shrugs, dabbing her lips with a paper napkin.

"We're expecting a crowd between Christmas and New Year's, but any time next week is fine. Just call first to be sure one of us is around." She gives Madelyn an appraising look. "So you're a photographer too."

"Too?"

"Meaning Fee, of course." She sweeps her hand at the walls."

"This is Fee's work?"

Kent shakes his head in fake disgust. "How like her not to tell you. Felene Orbison is one hell of a photojournalist, now retired. She's won a number of awards, notable among them a Black and White Spider Award for her work in Haiti in 1986. I'm sure there must be a copy of her book, *Paradise in Peril*, somewhere in Hayes Cottage."

"I had no idea," says Madelyn. "She seems so—"

Suddenly Jo Patton's face brightens. "Excuse me," she says and hurries off. All three turn toward the recipient of Jo's smile, a man in jeans and sport coat, his white shirt open at the throat.

In years to come Madelyn will recall a curious suspension of time, a brief pause in the earth's rotation during which she observes with detachment the breadth of his shoulders, his easy grace. Even from across the room she senses the force of his magnetism—an attractive man in his forties, secure in his masculinity and centered in his life. Then he laughs, his chin thrust upward, and time hurtles forward with dizzying speed, leaving her breathless, rooted in air. In this era of space exploration and cybertechnology, of international terrorism and staggering national debt, her entire vocabulary consists of only one word:

Adam.

Her first instinct is to flee to the bathroom. To the kitchen. To the deck to the steps to the safety of darkness to the sandy stretch between here and Hayes Cottage. But she is too late, for Jo Patton has taken Adam's hand and is urging him toward Madelyn, whose knees promptly lock, pinning her in place. Heat surges upward, erupting across her neck and cheeks.

He sees her then, his blue eyes registering a momentary flash of—what? Confusion? Regret?

"Adam, I'd like you to meet—"

"Maddy McCandless," says Adam Devlin, his implacability restored. He takes her icy hand in both of his. "We have met."

"You look wonderful," Madelyn manages to say.

"And you," he replies. How can she have forgotten the way his smile crinkles the corners of his eyes before spreading to his mouth?

"She's staying at Hayes Cottage," Jo says, turning to

Madelyn. "Isn't it a gem?"

"Delightful. A perfect hideaway."

"From what are you hiding?" asks Adam. He slips an arm around Jo's shoulder.

"My job, I guess. I've taken a temporary leave of absence." Not to mention my senses, thinks Madelyn, setting her empty wine glass on a nearby table. "And what brings *you* to Cypress Key?"

Adam's laugh lacks sincerity. "I live here," he says with a small shake of his head. "It just happened."

"So how do you two know each other?" asks Jo. The suggestion of a furrow invades her pretty brow.

"Ohio State," Madelyn says. "Eons ago."

"Twenty-two years," he says. "My God, Maddy, it's been twenty-two years!" His surprise is genuine.

"Are you still sculpting beautiful things out of wood?"

"In a manner of speaking, yes." A light goes on behind his eyes. "A forty-five foot schooner. *Osprey's* teak deck should be finished this week. She's a beauty if I do say so myself. You'll have to let me show you."

Madelyn's thoughts spin backwards to a farm in Ohio, where, in exchange for "no shenanigans" and a promise to "paint up" her house, old Mrs. Falter allowed Adam to live and work in her unused dairy barn.

"You'll have to let me show you," he had said then too, his beautiful, deft hands agitated with enthusiasm. She remembers the warmth of his hips between her thighs, her arms hugging him tightly from behind as the motorcycle raced across the winter countryside. She can still hear the roar of its engine augmented by snow banks, still feel the stinging cold, the thrill of speed, the flexing of his torso as they leaned into the curves.

The windows of the old cattle shed, fogged over by the cold, had cast perfect north light on the head of Adam's dragon, its body and tail still imprisoned in the twisted stump of apple wood rescued from his landlady's scrap pile.

He lived at the far end of the shed in a small, solitary room, accessible only upon invitation. Madelyn spent most weekends of her final semester at Falter Farm, sharing soup and sandwiches while they studied philosophy or huddled near the old wood-burning stove and talked far into the night. But always he would transport her home to the third-floor walkup she shared with Marisol Baya.

Except for once.

"I see everyone has met," says Fee, kissing Adam on the cheek. She looks around the room. "Who in hell *are* all these people anyway?" She laughs up at her companion, a handsome black man with a shaved head and horned-rimmed glasses. "Ben, what say we get a bullhorn and disperse all these louts." Clearly, Fee has enjoyed her share of champagne.

"Ben Waite," he says, offering Madelyn his huge hand. "I try to maintain the law around here. Some days are easier than others." He gives Fee an affectionate squeeze.

"Hard to imagine crime happening here in paradise," Madelyn says. She is drawn to this man whose presence seems to command the very air about him.

Ben Waite runs a hand across his head and offers her an engaging grin. "We have our share of trouble-makers," he says. "Petty thieves. Domestic squabblers. Drunks and idiots. Just last week we nailed two brothers waiting for the Tampa bus with $12,000 worth of cocaine wrapped up in Christmas paper."

Move and you're dead! Madelyn feels the color drain from her face, wishing with all her heart she could shake the memory of that terrible whisper.

During these deliciously carefree days on Cypress Key, she has begun to worry less about her health, her troubled daughter, her marriage. Even the attack in the garage has begun to feel remote, like scenes from some surreal film imbedded in her memory. But she has moments, like now, when the fear and horror come surging back, destroying her newfound serenity. She manages a smile for Ben Waite, thinking *It's comforting to know you're here in case I ever need your help.*

At 4 a.m. she lies awake, replaying every word, every gesture of her brief conversation with Adam Devlin. What did his face not quite betray when he first recognized her? Guilt for treating her so shabbily? Considering his dismay at toting up the years, she doubts he even remembers. Was it shock at her appearance? Perhaps she's changed more than she thinks. Or is she, as usual, jumping to the most invidious conclusion? Maybe the look was pure admiration, pure pleasure in seeing her again.

"Yeah, right," she says to Boots, nestled at her side. She plumps the pillows and flings one arm across her eyes.

And what about Jo Patton, who lights up like a marquee when she looks at Adam. Does he feel the same way about her? Are they a couple? Or is she just a number on his long list of admirers—young, attractive women with undamaged bodies and no strings attached. She hugs her knees in Anna Hayes' single bed trying to imagine herself having an affair, feeling sick and horrified at the mere thought of undressing in front of a stranger. Even David's forgiving eyes make her cringe despite his reassurances. No wonder he enjoys the company of Tee Kemble, whom he insists is not his lover. She's tall and shapely and equipped with a pair of everything!

"Deal with it, Madelyn, you're damaged goods." She

throws back the covers, pads to the bathroom to down two aspirin tablets. Then she carefully curls herself around Boots' purring warmth and draws the blanket to her chin.

"What if he wants to see me again?" she whispers into one silky ear. "What am I going to do about that?" But Boots isn't talking.

Chapter 13
Saturday, December 20

Spreading his sleeping bag beneath a low-branched tree, he loosens his boot laces, aware of his breath in the cold night air. He decides to wear several layers and sleep with his hooded sweatshirt pulled up over his ears. A rustling in the undergrowth makes him wary. Are there wolves in West Virginia? He gropes for his blade, his eyes probing the darkness. Good blade, quick and deadly.

When a squirrel darts out from beneath a nearby bush, he flinches, then rocks against the cold to ease the grinding in his gut and to quell the flashes of green lightning that strobe behind his eyelids.

Christ, his back aches. Not used to traveling eight hours at a stretch. Give anything for a hit or even a beer—something to help him relax.

Shivering with cold, he rolls up his down-filled vest

for a pillow and hunches down into the sleeping bag. Day after tomorrow, he thinks. Only two more days to go.

Chapter 14

Sunday, December 21

The next afternoon, thunderstorms roll across central Florida emptying the beaches and churning up the surf. NOAA warns of a water spout sighted just west of Homosassa Springs—unusual for this late in the season.

Feeling cloistered and restless, Madelyn dons an old slicker hanging beside the kitchen door and, with her Nikon carefully packed inside a waterproof case, heads off in the direction of lighthouse point. Her photographer's eye delights in the silvery sea against its backdrop of somber sky. She strides along beneath scudding gray clouds, drawing deep breaths and licking the salt from her lips. Exhilarated to be alone on such a wild afternoon, she is tempted to throw off her clothes and wade into the gulf, propriety be damned. Once a strong swimmer, she is confident that if forced to swim for her life, she could still outdistance any rapist. Proximity to water gives her courage.

Ahead stands the old lighthouse, its occulting beacon visible in the darkening afternoon. She knows its history from reading Arthur Delaney's *Smuggler's Isle*, which she found among Anna Hayes' many volumes of local lore. How horrifying the hurricane of 1843 must have been when its 100 m.p.h. winds and twenty-seven foot surge struck without warning. Madelyn is eager to photograph the three buildings sketched in Delaney's book—a keeper's stone cottage, a ruined boat house, and the 98-foot light tower. If she's lucky, she'll gain access to the interior of the tower and take some pictures from the top.

Part of her wishes David were here to share these churning skies and tearing winds, but a small voice of rebellion cautions her that David's conservative nature would temper the reckless joy she is feeling in this moment.

A lone jogger approaches from up ahead, his poncho flattened against his body as he pushes against the wind. His strides are labored as if his shoes are weighted. Alert to his body language, Madelyn prepares to take flight at the first indication of threat. This is what that bastard has done to me, she thinks. He's spoiled the pleasure of solitude. She moves toward the rising tide as he veers in her direction, a prickle of alarm inching up her spine.

"Hello!" calls the jogger, and the wind carries his voice away. "Hello, there." She exhales, recognizing Fee's party guest, owner of the Harbor Inn, and dredges for his name. Kent something—Jacobs? Jacoby?

"Did Allison call you?"

"No, why?"

"We want you to come for lunch tomorrow." Kent's legs pump up and down in place like a drum major.

"I'd like that very much."

"Good. Make it noon." He grins at her, pulls the towel from around his neck, and wipes his face. "And bring that with you," he adds, indicating her camera. With a little wave, he jogs off in the direction from which he came.

Madelyn shivers in the chilly ocean breeze. The horizon has turned black, and tiny white caps whip the surface of the gulf. If she hurries, she can make it back to the cottage before the next squall sweeps ashore. She'll leave the lighthouse for another day. Cutting inland between two cottages, she jogs homeward on Beacon Point Road.

A motorcycle is parked in Anna Hayes' driveway. Madelyn hesitates, looking about for its rider. She quickly unlocks the kitchen door, relocking it behind her.

For a moment she stands motionless in the silent house, listening for movement. "Hello?" she says, her voice faltering.

She tiptoes to the living room and freezes. Beyond the large window she can see a man's shoulder as he sits in a deck chair facing the surf, his black boots propped on the porch rail. Madelyn steps back into the shadows, her body rigid with alarm. Abruptly, he stands and stretches, and weak with relief she recognizes Adam Devlin. She waits for her ragged breathing to ease, then hurries to unlock the front door.

"How did you find me?" she asks, aware of her flaming face.

"Everyone knows Hayes Cottage," he smiles. "As a matter of fact, I spent the better part of April right up there." He points to the newly shingled roof. "Bitch of a job—all those angles and joints. You got any beer?"

"Come in," Madelyn says.

"No, you come out."

She ducks into the powder room to run a quick comb through her hair; then she uncaps two beers and carries them to the deck. Offshore a shrimp boat waltzes toward the harbor, the drone of its engine rising and falling with each dip and curtsey of its nets. Nearby on the sand a small boy charges a flock of sea gulls, scattering them in a chorus of squeals. Adam's presence has, for the moment at least, banished the beast, and for that she is deeply grateful.

"Is that what you do? Roofing?"

"Only for friends." He tips the bottle, squinting at the dark clouds overhead. "Somehow I never figured you for a college professor. I pictured you playing tennis, growing begonias, raising a couple of kids."

"Just one," says Madelyn. "Yesterday was Jessica's twentieth birthday."

"God." He shakes his head, leaving the rest unsaid.

An Irish setter lopes down the beach, then veers off to investigate a hole someone has dug in the sand.

"Tell me about you," Madelyn says.

He shrugs. "I became an innkeeper for awhile. That's how I ended up on the island. My aunt left me the Harbor Inn when she died. It's a great old building, and restoring it appealed to me at first. But it was one step forward and two steps back all the way. Drained my resources. So I sold it to the Jacobys and bought a boat, the first of three. That's what I do—run a small fleet of sport fishing boats, mostly during tourist season. Off season I work on *Osprey*." He shrugs again. "It's not a bad life."

"No, indeed." She studies his profile as he leans forward, squinting into the distance. His black curly hair and deep sailor's tan lend his mature face a handsomeness that it lacked in his youth. For the first time she notices a tiny gold loop in his left earlobe and realizes he is very different from the Adam she knew at Ohio State. How

129

could he *not* be changed? The Berlin Wall has come down since then, she thinks, and both AIDS and terrorism are pandemic.

"I have this yearning," he says quietly, "an urgency that I can't quite explain—a sort of primal need to return to a place I've never been." He measures her with his eyes. "It won't let me alone. Is that crazy?"

"Maybe just a little. What place exactly?" *I am really here*, Madelyn reminds herself. *With Adam. We are together on an island in the Gulf of Mexico talking as if twenty-two years never happened.*

He smiles. "Just—I don't know. Somewhere out there." His hand sweeps the dark horizon. "I think it must be what hatchling loggerheads feel when they struggle from their sand nests and trek back to the sea. It's the whole reason for *Osprey*, for the years of work and sacrifice. She's the means, don't you see?"

"And when she's finished?"

For a long moment he looks seaward without replying, his forelock lifting in the breeze.

"Tobago," he says, finally. Then he grins. "I didn't know that until this very moment." Suddenly the old Adam is back—her laughing boy who loved a raccoon and played Bach on the five-string banjo—and a small, silvery flutter begins in the pit of her stomach.

"Why Tobago?"

He shrugs. "Why not?"

Madelyn recycles what little information she has learned about Adam's life: that his mother died when he was in high school and that his father owned an insurance business in Gainesville. But the important questions remain unanswered: Has he ever married? Does he have children? Why did he vanish twenty-two years ago? For reasons she can't explain, she knows that if she probes for details, he'll withdraw, so she grits her teeth and resolves not to ask.

They talk about last night's party, about Fee's house and photographs. He tells her about the crew of plumbers who fled from the ghost of Lily Eastman while he was trying to restore the Harbor Inn.

Madelyn describes her meeting with Minneola Jones and the packet of greenish roux she has kept in the refrigerator for the past three days. "She says I have 'the look' and that she has her work cut out for her."

"Don't sell the old girl short."

"Surely *you* don't buy into all that hocus-pocus."

"Let's just say I keep my options open. I've seen too many of her predictions come true to do otherwise." He swallows the last of his beer and sets the bottle on the deck beside him. "Mind riding on the back of my bike?"

"Not at all. Where am I going?"

"You'll see." He slips his helmet onto her head

fastening the strap beneath her chin. Then he mounts the black Suzuki and kicks up the stand.

She climbs on behind him slipping her arms around his waist. And suddenly she is Maddy McCandless again, straddling a thrumming beast of a machine, her arms wrapped tightly around Adam Devlin. He aims the bike west on Beacon Point Road, his tachometer redlining before each skillful shift. Maddy thrills to the roar of the engine, the blur of speed, and the tensing of Adam's torso. *After all these years, I've come full circle.*

He downshifts for the dogleg south and follows along the west side of Beacon Lake. A half-mile further he turns into a narrow driveway and stops beneath a shed in a pine-rimmed clearing. Maddy removes the helmet, and together they race through a sudden downpour to the shelter of the light tower's recessed doorway. Thirty yards away stands the keeper's stone cottage, its red-tiled roof slick with rain. An appealing house, she thinks, small and cozy with a chimney on either end. She has a sudden longing to live in this place, to laze in the hammock stretched between two saplings, or to curl up with a book in the upstairs dormer overlooking the gulf.

"Who lives there?" she asks.

"Some old recluse who prefers peace and quiet to nosey neighbors and traffic and God-help-us tourists—no

132

offense." He delivers his sideways smile. She shoves back her waterproof hood and aims her camera at the house, then decides there's not enough light for the shot she wants.

When the shower abates, Adam grabs her hand and leads her toward the beach, avoiding roots and puddles. The structure ahead, although built atop an old stone foundation, looks sturdy and utilitarian, not at all like the sketch of the ruined boathouse Madelyn remembers from *Smuggler's Isle*. Solar panels occupy one end of the aluminum roof while two huge skylights extend along the length. A heavy duty block-and-tackle hoist juts from beneath the eave over a second story loading door shut securely against the weather.

He steers her toward the south end of the long shed past a trio of sawhorses supporting two long wooden poles. In passing he runs a caressing hand along their length. "Nine coats of spar varnish," he says. "Only three more to go."

"What are they?"

"Main mast and foremast. Those coils of wire rope are the standing rigging—the guy-wires that secure the spars to the hull."

"This is where you're building *Osprey*?"

"Yep. But first I had to build the shed."

"And the 'old recluse' in the keeper's house doesn't mind?"

"Maddy, that's *my* house. I lease the property from the state of Florida in exchange for upkeep. It's a good arrangement for everybody: The state gets a return on its investment; I get a great place to live."

He rotates the combination of a padlock and thrusts wide a pair of aluminum double doors. Madelyn breathes the heady mixture of fresh sawdust, epoxy, and mineral spirits. Inside, illuminated dimly by the skylights, the black hull of *Osprey* rests in a custom built cradle. She is larger than Madelyn imagined, her graceful lines and expert joinery apparent even to a novice.

"Oh, Adam, she's beautiful! Can I look inside?"

He throws a switch, directing high-intensity lights onto the work area, then grips Madelyn's arm, steadying her as she mounts the wooden steps paralleling the ship's port side.

Although the teak foredeck has been pegged and sanded, the rest of the deck is as yet unfinished, covered by a temporary plywood walkway. Warily, Madelyn steps aboard, uncertain of her footing.

"She won't shift on you, Maddy. Go on. Take a look below."

She climbs down the companionway ladder into the main salon, amazed at the comfort afforded by such a small space. An oval teak coffee table sits before a semicircular settee covered in black canvas. Adam demonstrates how easily the table can be raised to serve as a dining surface. The small galley, outfitted with stainless steel sink, refrigerator, and gimballed propane stove, has built-in racks for plates, cups, and glasses. Madelyn sits in one of two fixed swivel armchairs and listens as Adam identifies the electronic equipment ready for installation in the navigator's station: GPS, depth sounder, radar, weather fax, radio, and computerized satellite navigation with digital charting software.

"And get this," he says with undisguised pride. He slips a CD into a built-in changer, and John Coltrane bursts forth from a pair of speakers mounted in the walls.

After inspecting the engine room and two comfortable cabins, forward and aft, they emerge again into the cockpit, surprised to find the clouds gone and the red glow of sunset visible through the skylights.

"She truly is a work of art," says Madelyn. "And you've done it all yourself?"

He nods. "Except for hanging the keel and installing the engine—I had help with those." The flush of excitement vanishes from his face, and the dreamy look returns. "In another couple of months she'll be ready to launch."

"And then to Tobago?"

"Not quite. Sails are expensive. I may have to wait awhile for those." He grips her hand as she descends the narrow steps to the cement floor of the shed. "But once that hurdle is behind me, I'll shake her down for a couple of weeks—"

"What does that mean, 'shake her down'?"

"Try her out, find the bugs, fix them."

"And then?"

"Then I'll sell my fishing boats. Rod Ambert's already made me an offer on the big one. If I'm careful, I'll have enough to live on for several years at least."

The perfect opening, thinks Madelyn, but do I dare ask? His warm hand in hers gives her courage, and she plunges ahead.

"All by yourself?"

He gives her an amused look. "If you mean will Jo Patton be going with me, not a chance." He picks up a stainless steel bolt from the wet grass and slips it into his pocket. "Jo's pretty and fun, and I enjoy her company," he says. "Smart, too. A very savvy business woman. She owns Gulf Shipping, one of the fastest growing companies in the southeast."

"I had no idea."

"That's one of the things I like about her. She never trots out her credentials." He pulls a curly wood shaving from Maddy's hair. "Jo has no interest in living the life of a vagabond sailor. Few women do."

"So there's nobody to share this dream with you—no family, no kids?"

He pauses as if considering, then looks directly into her eyes. "No family. No kids. Nobody."

She struggles to control her sudden, soaring joy. "Can we climb to the top of the lighthouse?" she asks.

He sorts through a jumble of keys on a ring and holds one out to her. "Are you up for 127 continuous circular steps?"

She grins. "I am if you are."

He shoulders open the recessed door of the black and white striped tower and gropes for a light switch. Madelyn shivers in the chill dampness emanating from the thick, stone walls. The circular oak floor, bare of any furnishings, stretches to a diameter of thirty feet. Beside the door a handrail and a set of iron steps wind upward into the gloom.

Adam grabs a Coleman lantern from a nail behind the door and lights it. "You first," he says. As they plod toward the top, he tells her the history of the place, much of which she already knows from her reading.

"This tower replaced the original one, which was destroyed in the great hurricane of 1843. It was first powered by an oil lamp, then by an arc lamp, which proved to be very expensive and unreliable, then finally in the late 1800s by an electric filament augmented by a Fresnel lens."

"What's that?"

"A sort of lens-and-prism system that magnifies and projects the light source."

"How far out does it shine?"

"About twenty miles depending on the candlepower. You're lucky the weather is clear because this tower is also equipped with a diaphone horn, which on a foggy day is loud enough to scramble your brains."

Once again she is transported back twenty years to Falter Farm—chilly afternoons and evenings when they huddled around Adam's Marvel Stove and read to each other from Keats or Poe or *The Communist Manifesto.*

As the spiral of steps narrows in the dim light from below she can feel the heat of her face, flushed partly from the climb and partly from the feelings such memories beget.

On the day she had loaned her car to her roommate, Maddy decided to walk the four miles to Falter Farm and had arrived, glowing with victory and the stinging cold, bearing her newly completed master's thesis in a gray manuscript box. Adam welcomed her to his room with apologies for falling asleep and forgetting to stoke the stove. She remembers how he pulled off her snow-sodden boots, loaned her a pair of wool socks, and wrapped her in a blanket. Then he fixed them both a mug of instant coffee laced with rum. She settled in his one comfortable chair while he and Dub shared the bed, eager for her to begin.

She read to him of Mary Wollstonecraft, whose progressive ideas had shocked and discomfited her 18th century readers. With painstaking thoroughness, Madelyn's paper traced the contrasts between Wollstonecraft and Rousseau—her feminist challenges to his antifeminist doctrines—and quoted from her various works, explaining their profound impact on the French Revolution.

So absorbed was she in her own words that she scarcely noticed when Adam rose to stoke the stove, to refill her mug, or to let Dub out into the night.

"What irony," her thesis concluded, "that Mary Wollstonecraft, author of *Thoughts on the Education of Daughters*, should die in childbirth, never to see her own daughter, Mary Shelley, become a gifted poet and author in her own right."

Adam applauded softly as she replaced the last page, and Maddy, realizing he had listened without interruption for nearly three hours, felt a surge of love and gratitude. When he held out his arms to her, she went willingly, and they lay together in the dark, listening to the crackling of the wood stove and the sigh of the night wind.

In the present darkness near the top of the lighthouse, Madelyn is glad that Adam can't see her flushed face as she remembers his deft, square hands on her body, his soft breath against her neck. He had loved her slowly, seeking to please her with each caress, each kiss, each murmured word. She would recall forever how he eased into her, how they moved together, savoring the rhythm of the dance until, like Eve in Eden, she cried out "Oh, Adam." And they wept together, clung together, slept.

In the frigid dawn they had ridden in tandem under a canopy of a hundred billion stars, a rose blush washing the eastern sky.

From her bedroom window she had heard him downshift at the railroad tracks, speed up the incline, and disappear over Sugarloaf Hill.

The next day he was gone.

Adam and Maddy ascend the last of the spiral steps, edge past the six-foot lens housing the occulting light, and crouch through a low door onto a platform girding the top of the tower. She inhales the salt air and tilts her face toward Venus in the southwest. A new band of thunderstorms march in silhouette along the western horizon against the last traces of violet and magenta. At the faint clang of a bell buoy, her heart constricts. *I am here with Adam*, she thinks. *All this beauty belongs to him.*

They stand apart, treasuring the moment and the easy bond they share. At last he reaches for her hand.

"I don't know what 'look' old Minneola sees in

you," he says softly, "but the one I see is just as lovely as I remember." He leans down, brushing her lips lightly with his. "All I can say is David Ives is one lucky son of a bitch."

Chapter 15
Monday, December 22

The man shifts his weight from side to side, enjoying the whine of the engine and the heat of the seat against his crotch. Clean points and a new battery cable have her sounding good for a bike with over 90,000 miles on her. Running cool, even though he's pushed her flat out for the last three days. Less than a quarter tank of gas left. He'll fuel up in Tifton, Georgia. After that, only a few hundred miles more.

He grins behind the face mask of his helmet, feeling powerful, in control. No more days of taking orders, of backbreaking work in the cold. He downshifts at the foot of a tall bridge, then begins his ascent, redlining the tach as the bike strains toward the top.

He remembers when he was nine and Buddy Kelly would sneak down from the upper bunk in C-Dorm after lights-out, how the two of them would huddle together under the thin blanket and plan their escape—to steal a couple of bicycles, ride to Marblehead, and hide out in Buddy's uncle's old fishing cabin. They would have done it, too, if Sister Henry hadn't caught them asleep in Buddy's bed and shipped the kid off to Toledo. He can still hear Buddy's sobs, see the palms of his hands splayed against the back window as the white bus pulled away. He tries to imagine how it feels to just stop eating, to picture how his friend looked at 60 lbs. the night he died.

For a long time after that, the locusts would come every time he tried to sleep. It was always the same—at first a little shift in his mind like the sigh of a screen door closing. Then right away, if he listened hard, he'd hear them start up—first one of them whispering, then ten more, then hundreds, all whirring together as they chewed their way across his brain. The pressure of their chorus in his head would build and build until he couldn't stand it anymore, couldn't think straight, couldn't help sobbing and pounding his head against the wall.

Bile of old anger rises in his throat when he thinks of Sister Henry's punishment for making such a "ruckus"—a week of "devotions" all alone in the dark cellar. Instead of praying for his soul, he had squatted in terror atop an old boiler listening to the rustle of rats and roaches. After seven days he had emerged unrepentant, a half-crazed atheist bent on revenge.

From then on, Sister Henry was always on his case. If he was late for mass, she'd haul his ass to Father Merkle and stand outside the confessional until he'd done his beads. If he didn't do his homework, she'd hand him a bucket of sudsing ammonia and order him to the latrine. Between Mama and Booger Mendel and Sister Henry, he'd spent so much time on his knees that they swelled twice their normal size and had to be treated in the infirmary.

"Hey, Kneecap," the kids would jeer, dropping into the doggy position. So he became "Cap," a taunt that pissed him off at first but that eventually lost its edge. Even Rollo and Joystick assumed it was short for "captain," and that was okay by him.

With a twist of the throttle, Cap sends the motorcycle surging across a bridge. Awesome, tearing along this warm Georgia highway with handgrips vibrating, engine snarling, and wind pressing his sweatshirt flat against his chest. The second best feeling in the world. He pats the inner zip pocket of his down-filled vest where he keeps the pouch with the spoon, lighter, and syringe and tries not to think about Joystick's screams. *Stupid asshole deserved the broken arm the cops gave him for trying to hide a stash of China White in a thermos bottle! Should have known every badge looks there first.*

SUSAN B. JOHNSON

Viewed through his helmet's face guard, the river below looks cool and inviting. First a burger, then a quick dip in the Willahatchee to douche off the last 200 miles of road grit.

Mentally, he counts the bills in his wallet—just under $175. That'll buy enough gas to get him to Florida plus a couple of hits if he's careful. Then he'll have to get creative.

Chapter 16
Wednesday, December 24

Maddy flings back the covers and, avoiding the hall mirror, pads downstairs to the kitchen in her bare feet. She pours milk for herself and for Boots, who winds about her ankles, purring his approval.

"Here you go, sweet old thing." She sets a saucer beside him on the floor and rummages in the freezer for an open pack of Marlboros. Then tilting her head to one side, she lights up on the gas burner and blows a stream of smoke toward the ceiling, dispelling excuses, anxiety, guilt.

"I have nothing for which to apologize," she informs Boots. "Adam and I are just friends." Yet the words ring false. Isn't she, in fact, relishing the magnetic pull of sexual tension between them? Doesn't she pan the gulf for the *Lazy Jack* through Anna Hayes' binoculars and leap with dry mouth and fluttering heart for the telephone when it rings? Apparently, marriage, motherhood, and twenty-two intervening years haven't mattered all that much.

She exhales toward the ceiling. Then why the cigarettes? Why the pacing, the restless thrashing about in the night? Guilt about David? Not a chance. If "the arrangement" allows her husband to travel freely with another woman, no questions asked, surely the same rights extend to her. She flushes the butt into the garbage disposal and shoves a slice of Minneola's bread into the toaster.

No, she admits. This anxiety is not about vows or thou-shalt-nots. It's about an acute crisis of confidence, a case of pure fright resulting from two separate causes: the assault and the teredo.

Maddy lifts her milk glass, then sets it down again. *I could never allow it.* Imagining Adam's weight pressing down upon her spins her back to the night of the rape and, in a way, violates her all over again. She sags onto a kitchen chair, forcing the horrible memories aside. She pictures Adam touching her, kissing her. She imagines his long artist's fingers slipping the lingerie strap from her shoulder, waits as he bends to kiss her breast. She sees his look of tenderness turn to horror, feels him recoil at the long ridge of scar tissue, the glaring, terrible void.

Accept it, she tells herself, biting down hard on her lip. Deal with it now. Making love with Adam, or David, or any other man is no longer a life option. She lowers her head onto her arms and waits for the nausea to subside.

At noon Fed-Ex delivers a fat envelope to her door. Even without her reading glasses, Madelyn recognizes her neighbor Gil Everhart's spiky, ball-point handwriting on the mailing label. She puts the tea kettle on to boil, purposely delaying the moment when she examines the contents. Will there be another threatening note? Will Gil have upsetting news concerning the police investigation? Will there be a letter from David?

Dropping a tea bag into a cup of boiling water, she settles at the kitchen table with a sigh, and reaches for her glasses. She slips a paring knife beneath the flap and withdraws a handful of envelopes bound together with a wide rubber band. Gil's brief letter is on the top:

December 22

Dear Madelyn,

Hope you've thrown your worry beads into the Gulf of Mexico and are enjoying surf, sun, sin, and solitude. Oh well, three out of four ain't bad.

Sgt. Steffan is on the job. Several times a day two guys in hats and dark glasses cruise the neighborhood in a tan Ford with antennae (who *can* they think they're fooling?) and yesterday a Lieutenant Cobb borrowed your key to check out the house. He wouldn't say what, if anything, he discovered.

Four inches of snow have fallen since midnight, and more is on the way. Your friend Wynn Skyler asked me to assure you that she'll have one of her men shovel you out when (if?) it stops. Wish I were there.

David left a message on my voice mail last Thursday asking how to reach you, but he forgot to leave his number, so I suppose he'll either try again or call Wynn.

Drop me a line when you get a chance. Life isn't any fun without you.

Love, Gil

Guilt weighs on Madelyn's conscience. Even though Sergeant Steffan has cautioned her not to reveal her destination *to anyone,* she could at least have informed David's office that she was leaving town for a few weeks. But she had been so immersed in her own trauma, so eager to put Belleporte and all its attendant fears behind her, that calling Kohl and Sumner had not even occurred to her. To add to her guilt, since arriving on Cypress Key, her thoughts have centered almost entirely on Adam. David must be mystified at least—maybe even frantic—over her uncharacteristic behavior. She makes a mental note to call his secretary, Phyllis Ames, later on this afternoon.

Folding the letter back into its envelope, she turns her attention to the others: her monthly statement from Ohio Trust and Savings, an official-looking envelope from State Farm Insurance containing a settlement check for the van, and two bills—one from Ohio Bell with overseas charges, and the other from Texaco. Texaco? There must be some mistake. She hasn't used her Texaco card in years.

She frowns at the four charges: three in Ohio—Westlake, Belleporte, and Cambridge—and one in West Virginia. How can that be?

She fetches her purse from the newel post at the foot of the stairs and hurries back to the kitchen where for the second time this month she empties the contents of her wallet onto the table. Just as before, it's all there—driver's license, faculty I.D., a copy of her new prescription from Homer Pritchard, insurance card, family pictures, plus three credit cards—Visa, Sears, and Shell.

But no Texaco card.

She remembers now that she kept it apart from the others in the little zippered pocket along with her voter's registration card. Since she so seldom used either one, she didn't notice the Texaco card was missing when she first checked to see if everything had been retrieved.

Grabbing the statement, she looks again at the charges as the hair rises on the back of her neck: Belleporte to Cambridge to West Virginia. *My God, he's got my Texaco card, and he's heading this way!*

"Fax it to me fast," says Neil Steffan. "But first read me exactly what it says.

Madelyn struggles for calm. "December 18, Westlake, Ohio, 3.8 gallons, Self-service, Premium Unleaded, $13.68. Below that it says December 18, Belleporte, Ohio, 4.3 gallons, Self-service, Premium Unleaded, $15.91. Then the same day, December 18, Cambridge, Ohio, 4.5 gallons, Self-service, Premium Unleaded, $16.88. And finally, December 19, Charleston, West Virginia, 4.2 gallons, Self-service, Premium Unleaded, $15.20. The total of the bill is $61.67.

"So the first charge was three days after the assault. What's the closing date on that statement?"

"December 19—five days ago. Why is he buying only four gallons of gas at a time? It took about twenty gallons to fill up my van!"

"I don't know, but I'm sure as hell going to find out. You stay alert and close to the phone.

"What's your cell phone number?"

"I don't have one. My phone was stolen along with my purse."

"Then you need to get another one. Don't forget to fax me that statement. I'll be in touch." The line goes silent.

Madelyn sits very still, feeling the red tide of anger rising within her. I do not believe this, she thinks. First he rapes me, then he stalks me across the country? She stands abruptly, nearly overturning her chair. Well, that's just not gonna happen!

She throws on jeans and a sweatshirt, slings her purse over her shoulder, and pedals off on Anna Hayes' bike toward town.

Fifteen minutes later she is ushered into Ben Waite's office at the back of a brick building that serves as both Police Station and Village Hall. He motions her toward a wooden visitor's chair from which he scoops a pile of file folders.

"Morning," he says, settling his long frame behind his desk.

"Thanks for seeing me," says Madelyn, panting slightly. Now that she is here, she doesn't know how to begin. *Just tell him. He's intelligent, experienced, and a friend of Fee's. You can trust him.* She draws a deep breath. "I'm pretty sure I'm being stalked."

Ben Waite rises swiftly to close his office door.

"Talk," he says.

So she does. She tells him about the attack in the garage, the anonymous telephone calls, the cryptic quote from Coleridge, and Neil Steffan's entreaty to get out of her house. She forces herself to speak calmly, fighting back the panic coiled like a rattlesnake in the pit of her stomach.

Chief Waite listens carefully, his fingers forming a tent beneath his chin. Only when she pulls the Texaco statement from her purse and hands it across the desk does his gaze disengage from her face.

He studies it briefly, then depresses a button on his intercom. "Step in here, will you, Paula?"

A tall young woman in police browns peeks around the edge of the door. "Chief?"

"Photocopy this, please. Then fax it to Sergeant Neil Steffan—S-T-E-F-F-A-N, Belleporte—with three 'e's'— Ohio, P.D. Make sure the cover message includes my name and all my numbers."

"Right, Chief," says Paula, shutting the door behind her.

Ben Waite walks to the window on the other side of his cluttered office. He stands with his hands in his back pockets, rocking slightly on his heels. Finally, he turns and gives Madelyn a reassuring smile.

"You did the right thing by coming here," he says.

"I need to replace my cell phone—fast."

He shakes his head. "Don't count on service out here. You're in a dead zone—unless you stand in the middle of the Seminole Bridge. That's why the police department still communicates by radio."

"Then I'm going to buy a gun."

He shakes his head. "Bad idea."

"But . . ."

"You a trained marksman?"

"No."

He sits at his desk and uncaps his pen. "I want you to think very carefully before you answer. Who, besides Steffan, knows you're here?"

"Only my neighbor, Gil Everhart. And Wynn Skyler, Anna Hayes' daughter."

"Not your husband?"

"No. He's overseas. We're separated." Chief Waite writes quickly on a yellow pad. "Kids?"

"No, my daughter and I are—temporarily out of touch. She's living in New Mexico.

"Not anyone at work?"

"No one. Please tell me what you're thinking."

"Would either Everhart or Skyler be likely to reveal your whereabouts?"

"Absolutely not. They're very concerned about my safety. They both repeatedly warned me not to give my address to anybody." Madelyn fidgets, her knuckles white on the arm of the chair. "You think he's coming after me, don't you."

Ben rummages through his desk drawers. "Long ago," he says, "I learned two things that make me very good at what I do." He abandons the drawer search and begins shuffling through his desk top. "The first is never to jump to conclusions. And the second—" The stacked files in his in-box start to topple, and he steadies them with both hands, then resumes his search. "The second is that most criminals are stupid, and stupidity always tilts the playing field." Finally finding a small tape recorder, he tucks it in his shirt pocket and leans forward on his elbows.

"Now this is the way it's going to go down. Number one, you will *not* buy a gun—too many inexperienced gun owners end up as victims of their own weapons. Number two, you will remain calm and alert and will notify me the minute you sense anything out of the ordinary." He scribbles on the back of a business card and hands it to her. "Here's my direct line and my home phone. Call me at any hour. And number three—you will let *me* handle this reptile." He rivets her with his eyes. "Believe me, I'll enjoy every minute."

Madelyn pedals back along the strand to Hayes

Cottage, a lump of ice lodged in her solar plexus. Yesterday this sea was her sea, those wheeling gulls hers alone. Since then the landscape has altered. Something venomous has crawled ashore, keeping her focused on where she steps, what she hears, and how far from the safety of Hayes Cottage she has strayed.

Up ahead an old man stoops to poke something with a stick. She watches, wondering what he sees in the sand— a jellyfish, perhaps, or a dying horseshoe crab. She scans the horizon, oblivious to the beauty of the blue-green gulf. Instead she searches for evidence of the dark and deadly shapes that move beneath its surface. A chilling breeze brings gooseflesh to her arms and an unwelcome whisper to her ears:

I'm coming, Bitch, I'm coming!

Chapter 17
Wednesday, December 24

Unsnapping the chin strap, he pulls the helmet from his head and runs his fingers through his hair. *Hot down here.* He bungees the down-filled vest behind the bedroll and pushes up the sleeves of his sweatshirt. *Gas up, grab a dog and a brew somewhere, and make the last ten miles by three.* Beneath the new beard, his face twists into a grin. *Then the fun begins.*

Chapter 18
Thursday, December 25

❝You should see what the Jacobys have done to the Harbor Inn." Maddy grips the receiver between cheek and shoulder, picking nervously at her nail polish.

"Let me guess," says Wynn. "Ball fringe on the toilet seats?"

"Almost. Lots of swagged curtains and wallpaper with butterflies. But to their credit, they treated me to a nice lunch—cold salmon in aspic—and afterward gave me free reign to photograph. It's a great old building. I'm pretty sure I got some super shots." Carefully, she affects nonchalance, not wishing to alarm Wynn. "Any chance you can break free and come down here for a few days?" She hears her friend hesitate and pictures strong fingers pressing against her temples.

"Don't I wish," says Wynn. "But I'm in kind of a

161

jam here."

"Like what?"

"My yard foreman is off on another bender, and I've been running the office and two Christmas tree lots with no field manager and only part-time help. I'm so far behind, I'll be working double time all next week time just to catch up." She sighs. "About every six months he does this to me—gets liquored up and goes AWOL—but then he comes back, hat in hand, swearing he'll make it up to me."

"You ought to fire his ass and hire someone more dependable." Maddy nibbles at a hangnail.

"I know I should, but the thing is, when he works, he's a dynamo. Hold on a minute, I've got another call."

Maddy grips the receiver in her right hand and presses down hard on her stomach with her left. The strain of withholding her fears about the stalker from Wynn is visceral, causing her bowels to rumble and her head to throb. But getting through another lonely Christmas would be hard enough on Wynn. What could she do except worry? Maddy clamps her teeth tight and vows to tough it out.

"I'm back," says Wynn. "Did David call?"

"Here?"

"Yes. He phoned me from Brussels the other day after a week of trying to reach you. He sounded worried."

"What day was that?"

"Let's see, you left on Wednesday the seventeenth. It must have been the same day because Wednesday is delivery day. I remember a truckload of Poinsettias had just arrived, and Cory brought the phone out to the potting shed."

"What did you tell David?"

"Only that you had taken a leave of absence and were spending a few weeks in Florida. I gave him your address and phone number. That was okay, wasn't it?"

"Of course," says Madelyn, who feels a sudden rush of guilt; she has not, after all, called Phyllis Ames, David's secretary. Nor has she given any thought to David for the last two days. "Did he say anything about coming home?"

"No, only that he doesn't like the idea of your being alone today. Neither do I, for that matter. Christmas should be spent with family and friends."

"But I—" Maddy pauses, then plunges ahead. "Wynn, so much has happened that I hardly know where to start."

"For instance."

"Well, first of all, remember I told you about Adam Devlin, my boyfriend from college? Well, he's here on Cypress Key."

"I'll be damned! For the holidays?"

"No, he lives here. He roofed your mother's cottage

last spring."

"He's a roofer? Oh, crap, I've got another call. Hold on."

While she waits, Maddy rehearses the answer to what she anticipates will be Wynn's next question. *No, we aren't having an affair—at least not in the usual sense.* It's true, she thinks, but there *is* electricity between us. After today I'll know better where we stand.

"Back again," sighs Wynn. "Where were we? Oh, yeah—you were telling me about this roofer."

Maddy laughs. "No, not a roofer. He was just doing a favor. Adam owns and operates a fleet of sport fishing boats. But his real love is *Osprey*, the schooner he's is building in the old boathouse out on Beacon Point."

"And?"

"And we're—getting re-acquainted." She rummages in the kitchen drawer for an emery board.

"Tell me Adam doesn't have tattoos and a pony tail."

Maddy laughs. "No, but he does wear an earring. Oh Wynn, I wish you could meet him. He's bright and funny and handsome and not at all like Vic Manolo." She feels her face flame, fully aware she is gushing like a teenager.

"We can all be grateful for that," says Wynn. She chooses her next words as if walking barefoot in scorpion country. "So what are your plans?"

"He's invited me for Christmas dinner."

"Oh?"

"Couple of old friends—I figured why not?"

"Why not indeed? Listen, girlfriend, I've got to run. You have a great time today."

"God, I miss you, Wynn. Merry Christmas."

At twelve-thirty, Maddy squeezes the back tire of Anna Hayes' old bicycle and decides to give it one final pump. If she avoids rocks and pot holes, maybe it will get her where she needs to go and back before going flat. To play it safe, she tosses the pump into the metal basket and goes inside to wash her hands.

On Monday, she decides, she'll take the bus to Gainesville and replace the van. That way she'll be able to run for it in case— She refuses to finish the thought. For the time being, self-propulsion is her only option if she is to avoid being imprisoned in Hayes Cottage. "You just go on about your business," Ben had said, "and leave this reptile to me." Easier said than done.

She slips her camera strap over her shoulder bandolier-style and pedals off toward the marsh.

Once past the northeast end of Lake May, the four-lane road narrows to two; a half-mile further on, the paved surface changes to blacktop, then to gravel. Madelyn dismounts, walking the bicycle the last 50 yards to the rutted dirt road leading back through the trees to Minneola's shanty. A spindly goat looks up from grazing and follows her to the front door.

Minneola doesn't respond to Madelyn's first tentative knock on the door, so she raps again more loudly, then steps back a few feet and waits.

"What you want, chile?" calls the old woman, appearing from the side of the house.

"Remember me—Fee's friend, Madelyn Ives?"

"Reckon so." She wipes her hands on her dirty apron and looks the other way.

Puzzled at Minneola's cold reception, Madelyn opts for flattery. "Fee was right when she said yours is the best bread in the world."

But the old woman is not appeased. "Why you not use Minneola's roux?"

"Well, I— How did you know?"

"You still got the look, same as before."

"Please tell me what you see."

Minneola squints up into the trees as if invoking the spirits. Then she toes the dirt before her, forming a rectangle. From her apron pocket, she draws a handful of dark seed pods and arranges them within the box, taking care lest they overlap. Madelyn watches as she points to each in turn, then directs the same gnarled finger at Madelyn's face.

"Minneola sees fire," says the old woman, squinting hard at Madelyn. "It's a warning."

"Of what?"

But the bird-like creature merely beckons, leading her inside.

Ten minutes later, Madelyn is pedaling back toward Hayes Cottage, feeling both reassured and foolish. In her basket is a loaf of fresh bread wrapped in paper towels, while tied to her left wrist is a whitened circlet of bone.

By two o'clock on Christmas afternoon, chill winds from the northwest have churned the black-green Gulf into a froth of whitecaps and spume. Maddy follows Adam's instructions, dressing warmly in layers. First heavy cotton socks, then jeans, then a cotton turtleneck under a cabled fisherman's sweater. For good measure, she stows a windbreaker into her carryall alongside her portfolio of lighthouse photographs, which she plans to show to Adam—or maybe not. Then she paces, dragging impatiently on a Marlboro and checking her watch. What can be keeping him?

When Adam still has not arrived by three-thirty, she peels off the sweater and turns on the Weather Channel. More snow in the Great Lakes region, rain in the Southeast.

Her eye measures the distance on the weather map from Florida to Ohio, a world from which she feels increasingly estranged. Mentally, she tours the house in Willow Park—the living room with its bright pillows and hardwood floors, the sunny kitchen, the two-car garage—ugh! She mutes the TV and grabs the telephone on the first ring.

"Where *are* you?" she asks Adam.

"In Amsterdam," David says. "Where in hell are *you*?"

Maddy flushes. "Oh, David! I thought you were— Is everything okay?"

"Of course." His voice is neutral. "You're certainly a lady on the go these days. I've been trying to catch you for over a week."

"I know. We keep missing each other. Are you enjoying the holidays?" This is idiotic, she thinks. Tiptoeing around each other like strangers. But we *are* strangers, each with a distinct other life. She looks around Anna Hayes' tiny living room, trying to imagine David stretched out on the rose damask couch or reading in the slipper chair by the window, his feet on the ruffled ottoman.

Out of the corner of her eye, she sees something shift beyond the glass, and freezes. Was it a face? She is almost sure it was a face. She steps as close as the telephone cord allows, her pulse pounding in her throat. Who could have been looking in at her?

"How long do you plan to stay in Florida?" David asks.

He wouldn't walk right up and look in the window, would he? "I'm not exactly sure. Does it matter?" Despite her distraction, she senses David's equivocation, sidestepping, politesse.

"Not really, as long as you're enjoying yourself."

She hears him draw a breath, recognizes the signal, and braces for his next words. "I'm returning to the States in a week or two. Thought we might—I don't know—give it another shot."

Could I have imagined someone looking in at me?

She forces her attention back to David. "I'm sorry, David. What did you say?"

"I said I'd like to try again. Madelyn, are you all right? You seem so fragmented."

Not long ago, her heart would have opened to his suggestion. Now she feels herself pulling back from him, forestalling him with her own neutrality. "Let's think about it," she says, "and we'll talk when you get back." Warily, she stares hard at the window, alert to any movement on the other side of the glass.

David clears his throat. "Heard from Jess?"

"A card just last week. She's dating an Indian."

"Jesus."

"We can't worry about her, David. She's twenty years old. We've got to step back and let her live her own life."

"When has she ever done otherwise?"

The sound of Adam's boots on the back deck rescue her from both her sudden fear and a conversation she and David have had a hundred times. "I've been invited for Christmas dinner," she says, "and my ride just arrived."

"Wynn tells me you've made friends down there."

"Yes. Sorry to cut this short, but I've really got to go."

"Well, then."

"You have a Merry Christmas."

"Madelyn?"

"What?"

"Oh, the hell with it. I'll call you next week."

Limp with relief, Maddy flings open the kitchen door and draws Adam inside, hugging him tightly.

"Whoa!" he says. "What's this?"

She breathes in his scent, rich with strong soap, salt air, a hint of fish from his windbreaker, and fights back tears.

"Christmas," she lies, wiping her eyes. "I always

turn to mush. You didn't see anybody lurking around out there, did you?"

"Just me," he grins. "You expecting somebody else?"

Half an hour later they have offloaded their gear from Adam's pickup and stowed it aboard the *Lazy Jack*. By five o'clock they have cleared the harbor and headed out around the lighthouse on Beacon Point.

Excited by her first sea venture, Maddy sits on a tall swivel seat hugging herself and watching Adam's deft hands move from wheel to throttle to depth sounder. She is glad for the engine's roar isolating them from each other, preventing easy conversation. For she doesn't want to talk just now—only to feel the power of the sport fishing boat as it plows across the water and watch the receding shoreline. How thrilling this world of dolphins and cormorants. How removed from Belleporte, Ohio.

He can't find me here. Not while I'm with Adam.

As they round Beacon Point, Adam heads east, lifting a finger toward a small island dead ahead. "Owl Key," he shouts.

The wind has tousled his black hair, falling willynilly across his forehead as it must have done in childhood. Maddy tries to envision him at five—stubborn, no doubt. Perhaps a bit too serious. She thinks of her own child, beautiful and angry, whose hair once cascaded in waves to the middle of her back. As is often the case, thoughts of Jessica cause her stomach to knot, and she wills them away, determined to let nothing—nothing!—spoil this evening.

Adam maneuvers *Lazy Jack* between two buoys marking a narrow cut in a sand bar on the lee side of Owl Key, then eases across the shallows, bringing the starboard fenders to rest alongside an old concrete dock. Maddy watches as he secures the bow and stern lines to a pair of rusty cleats, locking down each with a hitch and flemishing the ends of extra line.

They unload a picnic hamper, a cooler, and a couple of canvas tote bags and pick their way through weeds and broken concrete toward the beach.

"Does anybody live on this island?" Maddy asks.

"Not since Lyle Odum died about fifteen years ago." Adam chuckles. "Used to stand out on his dock with a 12-gauge shotgun threatening anyone who tried to come ashore. Folks were sure he was hiding something—a still, maybe, or a crop of marijuana." Adam points toward the treetops. "Found him up there where his old tree house used to be. Dead about two months. Just a crazy old man with a few books, a couple of kerosene lamps, and a preference for privacy." Adam grins at her. "Sometimes I envy him."

At dusk he spreads a blanket on the sand, lights a

lantern, and pulls a bottle of wine from the cooler. "Hungry?"

"Starving," says Maddy. She sits cross-legged on the blanket, her hands in her jacket pockets. "Who owns Owl Key?"

"The state of Florida. It's a wildlife preserve. We're trespassing." He hands her a paper cup, then lifts his own in salute. "Merry Christmas, Maddy McCandless."

"I can't think of a single place I'd rather be."

"Nor I," he says, leaning over to kiss her lightly, then lies back on the blanket. "When are you going to come clean?"

"About what?"

He crooks one arm behind his head. "About you and David. Why aren't you spending Christmas with him? Or with your daughter?"

"We're separated. All of us." Maddy instructs her face not to flush. "We needed some time out."

"So it's temporary?"

She unlaces her right shoe. "I thought so at first. Now I'm not so sure."

"Because?"

She hesitates, framing her answer carefully. "Because I am not the person I used to be."

"That's odd. I think you are *exactly* the person you used to be."

"My very point," she says. "In the last month I've begun to get myself back, the self I almost lost while giving little dinner parties and attending P.T.A meetings and grading student essays." She empties sand from her shoe and reties the laces. "I like me better this way." She smiles at him and threads her fingers through his. "When are *you* going to come clean?"

"About what?" He sobers. "Oh, you mean about Ohio State."

For several moments he says nothing as if gathering his thoughts. Then he sits up and fishes a small package from his jacket pocket, placing it in her hand.

"A peace offering," he says, meeting her eyes. "And an apology."

Holding her breath, Maddy removes the brown wrapping paper, opens the lid of the small box, and leans into the glow of the lantern. Beneath a layer of cotton, a tiny carved raccoon face looks back at her, its beady eyes ringed with black.

"It's Dub," she says softly, her voice catching. "Oh Adam, he's beautiful." Only then does she realize that the wooden image hangs from a slender gold chain. She hands it to Adam and turns away, sweeping up her hair so he can fasten it around her neck.

"I took him with me to Gainesville," he says. "It was

amazing how quickly he bonded with my father. Followed him around. Slept at the foot of his bed. When Dad died, Dub spent several days poking into closets looking for him." Adam shakes his head, remembering. "Used to give me this disgusted look as if to say, 'What have you done with him?' The same day I sold the house I found him dead in the garage. Poisoned. I never found out who." Adam's mouth works in emotion. "That was the winter I lost everybody I loved."

Maddy lies next to him on the blanket, pulling his head against her shoulder. After a moment he continues, his voice rock steady.

"I can't tell you what you want to know because I don't understand it myself. All I can say is that when Dad died and Dub died, something died inside me, too. I felt rootless, scared. Everything I touched turned to shit—my plans for college, renovating the Harbor Inn. By the time I began to pull myself together, you had married David." He shakes his head. "I blew it."

"All these years I thought you must have found somebody else."

"Nobody else," he says, rising on one elbow to face her. "No one."

She smiles, fingering the carving. "Thank you for my Christmas present. I'll wear it forever."

After a meal of cold Rock Cornish game hen and

asparagus vinaigrette, they walk hand in hand along the narrow strip of beach to the north end of Owl Key. The tide is out, uncovering the broken remains of an old breakwater on which they stand with their coffee to watch the last streaks of gray twilight recede into night. They can see the lights of Cypress Key winking a quarter-mile across the water, but here on Owl Key only the lacy white edges of the waves are visible in the gathering dark.

"I've loved every minute of this evening with you," says Maddy softly. "Nine months ago I couldn't have imagined such contentment."

"That would be—March. What happened in March?"

She drew a breath. "Cancer happened," she said. "Chemo. Radiation. The works." There, she thinks. Now he knows.

"Sonofabitch" he says softly. "And now?"

"So far so good."

He thrusts his hands into his pockets. "My mother had ovarian cancer," he says. "She refused treatment. I've never forgiven her for that."

Suddenly, on the opposite shore a fire flares, then another and another. Black figures can be seen running back and forth stoking the flames, which climb higher and higher, sending sprays of sparks up into the blackness.

"What is it?" asks Maddy in alarm. "What's burning?" *I see fire*, Minneola had said—*a warning.*

But Adam chuckles. He sits beside her on the sand and pulls her close. "That'll be Ed Meeks and his boys—right on schedule. They own the only Christmas tree concession on Cypress Key, and every Christmas night the islanders gather on the strand as the Meeks family sets fire to the leftovers. Listen."

To her delight she hears the faint strains of "Hark, the Herald Angels Sing" borne on the breeze across a quarter-mile of water and on out to sea.

Chapter 19
Friday, December 26

E asier than he thought, finding her place out on the beach. And perfect for his plan—isolated, no street lights. Bitch almost saw him peeking through her window, but how else could he be sure?

Cap runs his tongue across his dry lips. This time he'll show her how it's done. This time he'll get it right.

He gives the throttle a little goose, then skids the motorcycle to a stop in front of Pépé's Bodega, spraying gravel. His eyes sweep around the parking lot. No black pickup with flames along the side. Not a good sign.

He turns the bike toward the highway and sits astride, letting her idle. For once the locusts lie quiet behind his eyes, and he can see in all directions. Got to be real alert buying smack from a stranger, especially in a piss-ant place like Cypress Key. Especially from a woman.

But the word on the street is that Elva Paston cuts the best deal for the best stuff. And right now he has a need for the purest that $100 can buy.

After that, it's gonna be just him and the bitch.

After that, it's gonna be party time!

Chapter 20
Saturday, December 27

First things first, Maddy thinks. Holding a match to her third cigarette since breakfast, she inhales deeply and reviews her list:

> set up camera
> buy security timer, cat food, cigarettes
> deposit insurance check
> arrange for ride to Gainesville
> postpone session with Fee

She grimaces, underlining the last item. Madelyn hates missing an opportunity to spend the afternoon with Fee, especially since she knows such invitations are rare.

Wynn had been incredulous when she called with the news. "Are you telling me she's invited you into her studio—her inner sanctum? Mad, I don't think you understand how extraordinary that is. Nobody *ever* gets that close to Felene Orbison. She protects her privacy like a lioness!"

But there was the proof scotch taped to the refrigerator door.

Come on over any time after three. And dress warmly. My studio's like a crypt.

Fee

In the short time they have known each other, the two women have developed a friendship that exceeds their mutual interest in photography—a closeness based on humor, trust, and respect for each other's privacy. So why do I dread explaining this mess to Fee when clearly she deserves to know? she wonders. Why is it so difficult to admit how frightened I am of this maniac? Reluctance to appear the victim? False bravado?

No, she decides, dumping her cold coffee into the sink. *It's because telling Fee about him gives him recognition and allows him access to my life.*

As she reaches for the receiver to make the call, the telephone rings. Adam, she thinks, softening her voice. "Hello?"

On the other end of the line she hears someone stir as if shifting the phone from one hand to the other. Then nothing.

"Who is this?" She listens intently for background sounds, for breathing on the other end of the line. Someone is there. In the familiar silence she senses a presence that relays fear along every taut nerve in her body. "*No,*" she had whimpered from the cold garage floor, "*please don't.*" But the animal had kicked her, torn at her body as if it were so much carrion. Madelyn grips the receiver with both hands, her fury surging.

"Listen to me, you sonofabitch," she yells. "You come near me and I'll blow your head off!" She slams down the receiver, then braces herself with both hands against the counter to quell the nausea. He's found me, she thinks. He's here on Cypress Key 800 miles from Ohio. She leaves a message urging Ben Waite to call, then cups her hands beneath the tap and leans her face into the cool water.

Maddy unzips the case holding her back-up camera. She mounts the Pentax on her tripod and angles it through the kitchen window, bringing into focus the step ladder, a temporary target straddling the back doormat. *One click is all it takes*, she thinks. *I may have promised Ben not to carry a gun, but I can still shoot if that creep comes anywhere near my door!* A rush of adrenaline energizes her. Taking action feels good.

She returns the ladder to the carport, locks the house, and pedals off toward town on Anna Hayes' bicycle, keeping close watch on the new rear view mirror clamped to the handlebars. No cars follow her. Fewer than usual approach her heading for the beach. In her straw hat and sunglasses, she feels anonymous and somewhat protected.

Fifteen minutes later she parks the bike behind the pool house and enters the Harbor Inn through the side entrance. Billy Vine, the front desk clerk, lifts his eyebrows in recognition.

"Afternoon, Ms. Ives. You here for tea?"

"Not today, Billy. Mr. or Mrs. Jacoby around?"

"The very person you seek," says Kent's voice behind her. He drapes an arm about her shoulder and gives her a sideways hug. "Was Santa good to you?"

"Why, yes," says Maddy with a smile. "As a matter of fact, that's why I'm here."

Kent contrives a pout. "And I thought it was because you find me irresistible." He steers her toward a brocade love seat.

"That too, of course. Actually, Kent, I've come to ask a favor."

"Anything at all."

"I need a ride to Gainesville on Monday, and it occurred to me that the inn must provide limousine service to the airport."

Kent barks out a laugh. "If you can call Billy's old Buick station wagon a limousine. You're leaving us so soon?"

"Not leaving. Shopping. I need to buy a car."

"Santa *was* good to you!" says Kent. "What kind?"

"Not another van, that's for sure." Omitting the grisly details, she tells him of the stolen van and mentions the insurance check that arrived three days ago on Christmas Eve. "I want something small, reliable, and relatively inexpensive."

A grin spreads across his face. "Lady, this is your lucky day." He pulls her to her feet. "Follow me."

He leads her back through the kitchen, redolent of fresh-baked apple pie in preparation for the early seating. Pausing to collect a key from a nail, he opens a side door leading to a combination storeroom and garage and flicks on the overhead light.

"Voila! Small, reliable, and relatively inexpensive!"

Maddy flushes with delight. "It's so—red! What is it?"

"A 2012 Mazda Miata with only 1,500 miles on her. CD Player. Removable hardtop. A little sweetheart I bought for Allison as a birthday present. She hates it."

"Why?"

"Manual transmission. She refuses to learn. Can you

handle a stick shift?"

"I could twenty years ago. But won't Allison—?

"Believe me, she'll be grateful if you take it off her hands. What she really wants is a van."

Maddy shudders inwardly. "Can we go for a test drive?"

"*You* can," says Kent, glancing at his watch. "I have a group of guests arriving any minute." He raises the garage door and hands her the key. "Go ahead, have fun. But check the fuel gauge; you may need gas." He waits while she buckles the seat belt and adjusts the mirrors, then waves her on her way.

Two hours later Maddy parks her new Miata beside the patrol car in Anna Hayes' driveway and quickly gathers up her purse and groceries. Ben Waite sits on the top step, his brow furrowed, his dark face etched with concentration.

"This is not a social visit, right?" she says. Without a word, he ushers her into the kitchen. She notices his curious look at the camera on the tripod, but feeling slightly foolish, she decides not to explain unless he asks. Quickly stowing a carton of eggs and a quart of milk in the refrigerator, she sits across from him at the kitchen table, one foot tucked under like a child. The stench of bad news pervades like sewage.

"Tell me," she says. "Whatever it is, just say it."

Ben removes his sunglasses and pinches the bridge of his nose. "HOGS," he says. "At least twenty of 'em. Started arriving yesterday morning. Neil Steffan and I agree you need to be on the alert."

"Hogs? What hogs? I don't—"

"The Harley Owners Group of Springfield," he explains. "Motorcycles with Ohio licenses all over town." He leans forward on his elbows. "Steffen and I are pretty sure that somebody riding a big bike like a Harley-Davidson charged four tankfuls of gas to your Texaco card."

Maddy looks at him, stunned. "What makes you think so?"

"Deduction, research, arithmetic, and guesswork. Mostly the latter." He flashes her a smile, banishing the tight lines around his mouth, then grows serious again as he draws a small note pad from his shirt pocket. "Low- and mid-priced Hondas and Yamahas and Harleys generally have smaller tank capacities. I happen to know, for example, that the Harley-Davidson Sportster holds just over 3 gallons. Multiply that times two bucks a gallon, and you've filled the tank for about $7." He studies the figures on the note pad. "But Mr. Texaco spent an average of $8.83 a pop. Bigger tank, bigger bike."

"So you think he's—"

Ben stays her with a hand. "Just let me finish. A smaller bike traveling at 65 m.p.h. will get 170 miles—max—per three-gallon tank. Unless, of course, the guy's toting an extra gallon in a can, which would then approximate the capacity of a larger bike."

"You've lost me," says Maddy, shaking her head.

"Put simply," Ben says, tapping the note pad, "from this information we can *not* exclude the possibility that he's riding a Harley-Davidson, and today twenty of 'em roared onto Cypress Key."

"Vic Manolo was always talking about buying himself a used Harley and fixing it up." Maddy hugs her abdomen, feeling sick with foreboding. "So what do we do now?"

"For starters, my men and I are going to keep close tabs on these guys. Good thing about the Hogs—they're easy to spot, and they tend to stick together. Also, we're doubling our patrols of this area as much as possible, so don't be alarmed if you see my guys hanging around. I've already spoken with my friend Hank Corbin, who used to ride a Harley. He's agreed to talk bikes with some of the HOGS, see if he can find out where they've been and where they're going, that sort of thing." Ben checks his wristwatch. "I've got a meeting across town in ten minutes," he says. "Your job is to keep it together and to call the station immediately at the slightest sign of trouble. One of us can be here in under five minutes. Agreed?"

"I'm scared, Ben."

He seems to fill the kitchen when he stands. "Let me do the worrying," he says gently. "Just keep in mind how noisy motorcycles are. It's damned hard to sneak around on a Harley-Davidson."

Only after he has backed out of the driveway and driven off down Beacon Point Road does she remember that he had not returned her phone call about the face in the window on Christmas afternoon. And just now she was so rattled by his news of the HOGS that she forgot mention this morning's call from "the breather." She decides to wait until this evening, then call him at home.

Due to her purchase of the Miata and unexpected visit from Ben, Madelyn never got around to postponing her plans with Fee. And she is glad, for suddenly Hayes Cottage feels airless and confining. She stuffs her house keys into her Nikon camera case and sets off across the hundred-yard span of sand to Fee's house, where she finds her friend potting plants in the shade of a deck umbrella.

"Tell you what," says Fee, knocking her trowel against a clay planter. "While you get us some ice tea from the fridge, I'll finish up here. Then we'll get down to business."

Madelyn brings the pitcher and two glasses out onto

the deck. She sets Fee's glass on the umbrella table, then settles onto a canvas deck chair and wedges off her sandals. So soothing, this view of palms and beach and sparkling gulf. Surely evil can't happen in the presence of so much beauty. She leans her head back with a sigh and tries to relax.

"Would you like to tell me what in hell's going on?" Fee asks.

"What do you mean?"

Fee's clippers snip off an errant frond from an asparagus fern. "Did I just *imagine* a squad car parked in your driveway about fifteen minutes ago?"

"Oh, that," says Maddy. "It was Ben Waite with some information for me. Nothing important." She takes a long drink of her tea.

"So I'm supposed to believe that the Chief of Police, whom I happen to know is short-handed, takes time during one of the busiest weeks of the tourist season to deliver some unimportant information in person instead of picking up the phone?" She pulls off her gardening gloves and tosses them onto the umbrella table. "Sorry. I'm not buying it."

And suddenly it all comes gushing forth—the rape, the phone calls, the cryptic poem, the car chase, the Texaco charges, and finally the HOGS. Maddy is shaking so violently when she finishes that Fee, aghast, sits beside her and grasps both her hands.

"Mother of God," she says. "Why didn't you tell me all this before?"

"I felt safe here on the island. I just didn't want to believe he would follow me all the way to Florida."

"Does Adam know?"

Maddy shakes her head.

Fee gives her hands a squeeze. "Then you need to tell him, Maddy. The more people you have looking out for you, the less opportunity for trouble." She hesitates, then pushes on. "He's in love with you, honey. He'll be shattered if you don't let him help."

Just then the roar of a motorcycle brings them both to attention. They hear it approaching from the southwest along Beacon Point Road, see it thrust into view, slow down, and finally pull into Anna Hayes' driveway—a black bike with double side mirrors that glint in the afternoon sun. Maddy grabs her camera from the umbrella table and zooms in on the driver. She takes a shot of him as he balances the bike on its kickstand, then shoots again as he starts to unfasten the chin strap of his helmet. Suddenly, her camera goes blank. "Damn!" she yells as the man moves out of sight toward the back door. "My battery's dead!"

Fee yanks open her sliding glass door, seizes a pair of binoculars, and rushes back to the deck just as the cyclist reappears. She trains the glasses on him as he swings his leg across the seat, starts the engine, and roars off in the direction from which he came.

"Did you get a look at him?" Madelyn's voice strains with tension.

Fee shakes her head. "Black helmet, black shirt, black pants." She picks up Madelyn's digital camera and heads indoors. "We'll know more after we download these photographs."

In her studio Fee transfers Maddy's pictures to a file on her computer and opens it in Photoshop, quickly adjusting the levels, zooming in, and sharpening the edges. One shot is frustratingly unfocused, but the other clearly reveals the man's image.

"Ben's going to get you, you bastard," says Maddy through clenched teeth. After Fee's photo printer spits out both images, the two women settle side by side on Fee's black leather sofa to study the prints through a magnifying glass in the light of a halogen reading lamp.

"Lousy resolution," says Maddy, shaking her head.

"Better than nothing," says Fee.

The zoom lens has caught the man in partial profile, his helmeted head tilting backward as his left hand grapples with the chin strap.

"What's this," asks Fee, pointing to a symbol on the side of his helmet. "Can you make it out?"

"Looks like a shield or a crest of some sort."

In the other photograph, the shadow of the roofline conceals the man's head and left shoulder as he steps toward the kitchen door of Hayes Cottage. But this picture reveals a detail the other does not—a pair of light-colored gloves hanging from his back pocket.

"See that?" says Fee, pointing to the watch strap on his right wrist. "He's left handed."

"He's also about six feet tall, judging from that clump of seagrass next to him." Maddy slumps in disappointment. "Not much to go on."

"All the same, you need to turn these over to the police immediately," says Fee, pulling her friend to her feet. "Maybe they can detect something you and I have missed." She removes her reading glasses and reaches for the telephone. Suddenly, she stops, a look of awe on her face.

"I'll be damned! She's done it again."

"Who?"

"Minneola. That old woman read you like a book. She saw right away that you're in some kind of trouble. My God, no wonder she says you've "got the look!""

Chapter 21
Sunday, December 28

With his stash running low, Cap rides over to the mainland to scope out Easy's, where a guy down on the beach says he can connect. He orders a long-neck and sits at the bar, his eyes and ears open to opportunity.

After about fifteen minutes, a lonely-looking redhead sits down at the other end and orders a bourbon and gingerale. He watches her light a cigarette, then wanders over to make conversation and check out her arms for tracks.

"Hey, Red," he says, and she gives him that look they all use—that snotty "get lost, Bozo" look—but he knows women, knows how they always say one thing and mean something else. So when she turns away and starts talking to some asshole with a military haircut two stools over, he figures sooner or later he's gonna score.

This one—Nicki Alverez, she tells the uniform—plays it up, tugging her skirt down over her thighs and arching her back to show off her tits. She's wearing this fuzzy blue sweater with a little picture of a rabbit on it, and she smells like flowers—just like the other one did, the one in the garage.

He knows how the goddamn game goes. So he nurses his beer and waits. Hell, he can wait for an hour if she wants him to. He can wait all night, however long it takes.

When she slings her pocketbook strap over her shoulder and slides down off the stool, he figures she's going to the can, but instead she walks right out the door, and he recognizes the signal: It's his turn now.

She has to reach through the open window of her car, an old, beat-up Chevy Nova with no door handle on the driver's side, and she takes her sweet time looking for her keys before sliding behind the wheel. The trouble starts when he gets in beside her and reaches out his hand to pet the rabbit. Christ, can she scream! "Get out! Get out! Get away from me!" Calling him a creep and a weirdo.

Next thing he knows, two guys grab his arms and hair and haul him head first out of the car and start pounding the shit out of him while the redhead takes off like A. J. Foyt, spraying gravel.

When he comes to, he's pissed himself and there's blood all over the front of his vest. One of his teeth is loose, and his nose hurts like a sonofabitch.

Later that night, he lies in his sleeping bag holding a wet tee shirt against his face, trying to ease the pain, but the locusts won't let him sleep. A whole chorus of them is whirring out on the edges of his brain, whispering to him so soft that at first he can't make out the words. He wants to scream at them that it wasn't his fault, that the bitch asked for it by sitting there tossing her hair and tapping the ashes from her cigarette with those pointy, red fingernails. But his head hurts and he can't breathe through his nose and they won't stop whispering to him in those whirring locust voices. Won't stop gnawing toward the center of his head, getting louder and louder, telling him to kill her, kill her, kill!

He sees the sense of it—to make the redhead pay. Nobody prick-teases him and lives—not that little spic at Easy's and for sure not the snotty school teacher bitch! First he'll finish what he's come all this way to do and take out Madelyn Ives. He shivers in the dark, thrilling to the image of his razor-sharp blade slicing through white flesh.

Then he'll do Nicky Alvercz. Clutching himself beneath the covers, he feels the rage rise in his hand. She can kiss her pretty face good-bye.

Chapter 22
Sunday, December 28

Maddy parks her red Miata near the wharf in the inner harbor and tunes the radio to WUFT in Gainesville. She sighs as Beethoven swells from specially installed Bose speakers. Nothing but the best for Allison Jacoby. With the top down she can see not only northeast to the winking lights atop the Seminole Bridge but also southwest to the flash of the occulting light out on Beacon Point. At the top of that tower, Adam Devlin kissed me, she thinks, allowing herself a little shiver of pleasure. She checks her face in the rear view mirror. We're just friends, she cautions herself, no matter what Fee thinks. Keep it simple.

Dead ahead is the harbor mouth, through which at any minute the *Lazy Jack* will glide with its coolers of snapper and its sunburned tourists on the run from a northern winter. Like me, she thinks.

And what else is she escaping? She glances about the deserted parking lot, prepared to flee if any suspicious car—or worse, a motorcycle—pulls in. Feeling exposed and vulnerable, she quickly raises the convertible top and locks it in place.

Across the harbor clanging sailboat halyards lend dissonance to the "Emperor Concerto," creating a foreign world that she knows she would enjoy if only she could relax. She forces herself to think about the evening ahead, hoping Adam isn't too tired from the strain of the long hours playing host. The very thought of spending a whole day on a pitching deck in the hot Florida sun makes her stomach lurch. But she is glad for Adam that others disagree. For over a week the *Lazy Jack* has left its slip each day at 9 a.m. and returned eight hours later, its charterers full of beer and bravado. For Adam this has been both a blessing and a curse: On one hand the brisk business has bolstered his savings, but on the other it has prevented his progressing with *Osprey*—especially frustrating since the schooner is so near completion. Tomorrow, despite the press of his chartering business, he will drive to Miami to consult with his marine architect and a sail maker about sails for *Osprey*. Maddy knows he has already arranged to sell *Lazy Jack* and *Rogue IV* to Rod Ambert just as soon as

Osprey is ready to launch. And after that—

After that she'll have to make tough choices about David and Adam and the next phase of her life. This, as Jessica would say, is *now*; that will be *then*. Carpe Diem.

At 5:45 *Lazy Jack* motors through the harbor entrance and backs neatly into her slip. Maddy admires the rope-like muscles in Adam's forearms as he steps ashore with the bow and stern lines and quickly hitches them. Then he straightens, wipes a brown hand across his brow, and glances around in search of her. She signals him with her headlights. He responds by holding up five fingers.

As she watches the men gather their gear and debark, laughing and clapping each other on the back, a heaviness settles upon her like a pall. Only three more days until New Year's. Eventually, she'll have to return to Ohio. Yet somehow Belleporte no longer feels like home.

A new surge of anger propels her from the car. Bad enough that the bastard nearly killed her—he has also stripped her of self-confidence, causing her to burst into tears as Willene Herbert predicted, to be terrified of strangers and afraid to venture out alone. Like yesterday's episode at the Amoco station. She had filled her tank and was waiting in line for the cashier, when a motorcycle pulled in and parked at the pump behind her car. As she watched the rider dismount, remove his helmet, and prepare to come inside, she was gripped with such unbearable panic that she muscled her way to the front of the line, threw a twenty dollar bill on the counter, and fled out the opposite door, nearly gagging in fear. Maddy struggles to calm herself. At least now the police have the photographs of the biker in the driveway, for whatever minimal help they'll provide.

She watches two of Adam's passengers struggle up the ramp with a heavy ice chest while Ernie Shaver, the dock boy, begins hosing down the decks. In an odd way, Anna Hayes' cottage feels more like home these days, a safe haven in which Maddy can explore her talents as a photographer and her ability to think, act, and live independently.

Except for the face in the window.

And a breather on the phone.

She wills her heart not to race, her eyes not to brim. Hang on, she tells herself. Just hang on.

"Whoa," says Adam, kissing her cheek. "What's all this about?"

She offers him a watery smile and jabs her thumb toward the heavens. "Stars," she says, as if this explains everything. She reaches up to him, slipping both arms around his neck, and breathes in the scent of his sun-kissed flesh.

He hugs her tightly, then releases her, stepping back

to cast a skeptical eye at the Miata. "When you said on the phone you bought a car, I thought you meant a real one! You don't actually expect me to *ride* in this wind-up toy!"

Madelyn dangles her keys in front of his face. "If you behave yourself, I might even let you drive." She pulls the trunk release so he can stow his sea bag beside a crock pot and a bag of groceries.

"See you Wednesday," he calls to Ernie Shaver, who acknowledges with a wave.

Adam pauses for a final check of *Lazy Jack's* neatly coiled dock lines, then folds his long legs into the passenger seat. "Reminds me of that limerick about the fellow with the Austin—the one who had 'room for his ass and a gallon of gas—.' Sure is *red!* What's she run on— tomato juice?"

With a withering glance, Maddy backs out of the Inner Harbor parking lot, shifts into first, and peels off toward Beacon Point. Not once does she look in her rear-view mirror.

While Adam showers, Maddy gathers a centerpiece of thistles and sea grass for the table set out on Adam's back deck. She opens a bottle of Burgundy, lights a candle lantern, and stands back to measure the effect. This is just beef bourguignon between friends, she reminds herself, not a seduction scene. She blows out the flame and goes inside to toss the salad.

Twenty minutes later, when Adam emerges dressed in suntans and a white cotton sweater, he finds Madelyn half-asleep in the hammock, her bare feet tucked beneath her long denim skirt. He hands her a wine glass, lifting his own in salute. "That kitchen has never smelled so good."

"I promised you I could cook."

He leans down to kiss her. "And do you always keep your promises?"

Guilt stabs at Madelyn. She hears herself promising Dr. Carl Friedman to serve as head of the Medieval Literature search committee next semester, promising her mother she will meet her plane at the Cleveland Airport, promising David she will love him "for better or for worse."

"I try," she says soberly. "But it isn't always easy."

Adam inches onto the hammock beside her. "I had forgotten that about you," he says.

"What?"

"Your willingness to commit, to make promises to the people you love."

"Isn't that the test of love?"

"Maybe. But why must love be tested? Doesn't the need to 'test' a thing imply doubt about its authenticity?" He raises himself on one elbow and studies her face in the last of the evening light. When he speaks again, his voice is husky as if issuing from some unused part of his heart.

"Why can't we just love each other, Mad—here and now, without the impediment of promises?" He lowers his face to hers, kissing her gently at first, then urgently, closing his eyes against the darkness. She feels a surge of longing as he holds her close, and remembers, like a half-forgotten lullaby, how much she loved him twenty-two years before. A small sound of pleasure escapes her. It would be so easy to forgive him for leaving her and to love him again. She entwines her fingers in his thick hair and pulls his mouth to hers, enjoying the flare of her own desire as his hand seeks her inner thigh. But when Adam's fingers begin to move upward toward her missing breast, she feels herself grow rigid beneath the weight of him. Suddenly, she can't breathe, and fireflies flash behind her eyes.

"No, don't," she commands, grabbing his wrist. She manages to hold him at arm's length and roll away, nearly overturning the hammock.

"Maddy—why?"

She perches on the wooden steps where she hugs herself, rocking back and forth in the dark. After a moment he sits beside her and pulls one of her hands into his.

"What's wrong? What did I do?"

She swallows hard. "Nothing at all."

"I thought you wanted to."

"I did. And for a moment I was almost able to forget."

"Forget what? David?"

"That I'm damaged goods." She turns to him, forcing herself to speak the words. "I have scars, Adam. From my surgery. You can't imagine how terrible."

"How can you possibly believe that matters to me?"

"I don't think I could ever bring myself to let you look at me."

He enfolds her in his arms and kisses her hair. "Then until I can convince you how beautiful you are, we'll make love in the dark."

Out on the point the tide whispers against the shore as the night wind rustles the palms. Adam pulls off his sweater and drapes it around her shoulders.

"That's not all," says Maddy, drawing a breath.

"Tell me."

She struggles to steady her voice. "Not all my scars are visible—at least not to most people."

"What does that mean?"

She rises and lights the candle lantern, setting it on the step beside Adam. Then she sits again, hugging his sweater around her.

"Remember I told you Minneola said I have 'the look'? Well, what she sees when she looks at me is fear."

Maddy searches his face, a pleading in her eyes. "A man is stalking me, Adam, and I'm terrified of what he's going to do!"

Adam rises swiftly to his feet. "What man? Who else knows about this?"

"Ben Waite knows. And Fee. And the police back home." As rationally as she can, she tells him everything, including Ben's motorcycle theory. "At last count there are twenty-three members of the Harley Owners Group of Springfield, Ohio, here on Cypress Key."

"Holy Christ."

In spite of her resolve, Maddy's voice begins to tremble. "So just now when you—when we—something in me snapped, and I felt like I was back there on the garage floor, like it was happening all over again." She bites down hard on her lower lip.

Adam pulls her against him, breathing hard. She feels the rigid way he holds her and draws comfort from his anger. After a moment, she straightens, drawing a ragged breath.

"No way I'm leaving here tomorrow," he says.

"You have to. We can't all put our lives on hold just because of some nutcase. Ben has assured me he's got things under control." She wipes her eyes on her sleeve. "I'll be all right."

"Just the same—"

"Really, I'm okay now," she says, smiling thinly.

"No," he says, with admiration. "Not okay—incredible."

At seven-thirty Madelyn drives home with the top down, enjoying the bite of crisp morning air. The day promises to be cloud free, and she looks forward to setting up her camera equipment on the Seminole Bridge, which affords the best view of Turncoat Key, nesting grounds of the loggerheads. By two o'clock the sun should be westerly enough to provide perfect light. I'm getting good, she thinks. All but one of her recent driftwood shots were balanced, sharp, and artistically framed. Fee's promise to help her assemble her "island collection" into a book has given her new resolve. She chuckles. Maybe the lie she told her department head was really the truth after all. Won't Wynn be surprised when she hears about Fee's offer?

She breathes in the rich sea air as she drives along the strand. Already the shrimpers are out on the sparkling gulf, while the early shell seekers and joggers have laid claim to the beach. Soon Ernie Shaver will arrive at Beacon Point to take Adam to the airport.

Three days without him, she thinks. And two nights. Remembering the taste of his mouth, soft and aroused, sets off a thrumming in her solar plexus. She remembers how gentle he was that long ago night in Mrs. Falter's dairy barn, the only other night they shared.

Last night he was gentle too, after the terrible telling. He had given her a soft flannel shirt to wear and curled his body around hers in the oversized bed, careful not to trespass. He had told her about his childhood dream of becoming a pilot and his summers building model airplanes in his father's basement workshop.

"By the time I was fifteen, I had saved $245 for flying lessons by cutting grass and washing people's cars. But it didn't work out the way I planned."

"What happened?"

"Beth Hooper happened. Her family moved in next door that summer. She had long blond hair and slim legs and so many guys sniffing around her that I never even had a shot. All I could think of to do was buy her stuff—posters, records. Once I paid sixty bucks for a white teddy bear, which I watched her take along on a date with Lenny Davitz. By the time we graduated from high school, most of my flying money was gone."

Madelyn had pulled his arms more tightly around her. "When did you first decide to sail around the world?"

"In college. It's all part of the same dream, don't you see? Just another kind of flying."

Sometime late into the night she found herself telling him about Jessica—about her beauty, her willfulness and tantrums. How as a child she would set her jaw when disciplined, then go right back and deliberately misbehave again. "I've loved her for twenty years," Maddy heard herself say. "And for twenty years she's reviled me."

Adam had smoothed her hair from her face and kissed her gently. "How can anyone not love you, Maddy McCandless?"

She would always be grateful to Adam for putting her feelings before his own desire and simply holding her until she drifted off. For four hours she had slept soundly—no nightmares, no awakening in alarm. At six she crept from his bed and slipped into her long skirt, leaving the flannel shirt neatly folded over the back of a chair.

Now she turns into Anna Hayes' driveway, reminding herself to buy champagne to toast the New Year the minute he gets home—even if it's ten o'clock in the morning. And maybe some caviar, she thinks, as she tucks the Miata into the carport. She locks the convertible top in place, then slings her purse strap over her shoulder, stooping to collect Boots, who emerges from beneath the deck.

"Hello, you old darling," she says, nuzzling his neck. "I bet you'd like caviar too."

It is then that she lifts her gaze to the back of the house and gasps, freezing in mid-step. Instantly, she drops

Boots and rushes back to her car, her hands trembling so violently that she can hardly fit the key into the door lock. She backs out of the driveway, grinding the gears in her haste to get away. For in Day-Glo orange someone has crudely spray-painted across the width of the kitchen door a single word:

DIE

Chapter 23
Monday, December 29

Police Chief Ben Waite enters his office bearing two Styrofoam cups of coffee and a box of ginger snaps. He hands one cup to Madelyn and shoves the door closed with his foot.

"Let's not jump to conclusions," he says, pulling the cellophane from the box. "There can be other explanations."

She sits rigidly in his one visitor's chair, clutching her cup in both hands. Something has lodged in her throat that will go neither down nor up. "Like what?" she asks in a tight voice.

"A random prank, for instance. Every so often we get a rash of graffiti." He offers her a cookie, but she averts her face and waves it away. "I'll have my men check around to see if it's happened elsewhere in the

213

neighborhood."

"Why would anybody do such a thing?"

"Kids," he shrugs. "Confronted with a blank wall and a can of spray paint, they can't resist." He grins at her and dunks a ginger snap into his coffee. "Did it myself once."

Maddy tries to picture Ben at thirteen, sneaking up on her porch with a can of Day-Glo paint, but the image eludes her. Jessica, on the other hand, would not have hesitated. She smiles in return, tightlipped and wan as if smiles are out of season. Is he right? she wonders. Am I overreacting? Abruptly, she stands and crosses to the window.

Outside in the parking lot a blonde in tight jeans places a parcel on the roof of her car and unlocks the trunk. Maddy holds her breath as the girl stows the package, exhales when she safely slips behind the wheel and drives away.

In its nervous heat, her body bears the scent of Adam, a sweet muskiness that incites a riot of sensations. Two hours ago she lay in his bed wearing his flannel shirt, feeling his soft breath on the back of her neck. She imagines him now in the air over central Florida, sipping orange juice and reading the *Miami Herald*, and for an irrational moment she panics. *What if his plane goes down and I lose him for good?*

Officer Paula knocks twice, then peers around the edge of the door. "Ohio on line three, Chief."

Madelyn sits again as Ben punches the button for speaker phone. "Sergeant? Ben Waite here."

"Yes, sir," answers Neil Steffan.

"Madelyn Ives is also part of this conversation. Any developments on your end?"

"Update on Raven—uh, Joe Haven. He spent most of November at Erie Mental Health Center—apparently not for the first time. The staff wouldn't discuss his case, but his landlady told one of our officers that six months ago "Joe" was diagnosed bi-polar. Apparently, he functions normally as long as he takes his meds. He was released on Wednesday, November 26. A couple of weeks later—she can't remember if it was December ninth or tenth—he took off without telling her where he was going, and she hasn't seen him since. Seems he owes her rent for two months."

The lines deepen between Ben's eyes. He levels a hard look at the telephone. "What about the house? Anything going on there?"

"All quiet, sir. We've eased back on surveillance. What about on your end?"

"A possible lead on a biker," says Ben. "We're looking at some photographs of a Caucasian about five-ten or eleven, 165 lbs., wearing boots and a helmet with some kind of insignia—sort of like the Oakland Raider shield." Ben drains his coffee cup and tosses it into the waste basket. "Oh, and he's probably left-handed. Sound like anyone you know?"

"Not offhand, but send me copies and we'll see what we can come up with."

"Already on their way. The bad news is—he's not riding a Harley-Davidson. Friend of mine who knows bikes says it's way too small for a Harley, but the picture isn't clear enough to identify the make."

"So," says Steffan, "I guess Manolo's still at the top of the list."

"You're keeping tabs on him, right?" he asks Steffan.

"I tell you, the guy's elusive. But when we checked his employment application for references, we found a cousin, Marie Collins of Jacksonville, Florida, listed as next-of-kin. He may be heading for her place."

"That would be consistent with the Texaco charges."

"Right. According to neighbors, this Marie Collins is away until after the holidays. Jacksonville P.D. is keeping an eye out for Manolo just the same."

Ben studies the legal pad in front of him, his brow furrowed in thought. "Maybe we should be looking for *two* men—one who assaulted Mrs. Ives and another who stole her credit card."

"But that would make the second man's itinerary a matter of coincidence. How likely is that?"

"Not very," says Ben. "We also have a new little problem. Either last night or early this morning, someone spray-painted the word 'DIE' on Mrs. Ives' back door. At this point we're regarding it as a 10-59, but I'm thinking it's time for the three of us to do a little brainstorming. And I'd like to record it for future reference. Everybody okay with that?"

Maddy nods. She sits tall in her chair, feeling as if she might topple at any moment, and waits while Ben positions his digital recorder near the telephone speaker and checks to be sure it's operating properly.

"Feel free to jump in here, Steffan." He pushes the record button, turns his legal pad to a new page, and uncaps his pen. "Madelyn, I want you to set aside the idea of Vic Manolo for a moment. Instead I want you to visualize others you know back in Ohio—people you work with, for example—and try to think who else might want to get back at you for some reason. Maybe because they're jealous? Someone feeling snubbed or insulted?"

"Sergeant Steffan and I already had this conversation weeks ago. I can't think of anybody."

"Give it your best shot," says Ben. "Anybody at all."

Madelyn bites her bottom lip, then slowly shakes her

head. "My department head wasn't pleased that I applied for sabbatical leave. Still, I hardly think—"

"Name?" asks Ben, his pen poised.

"Dr. Carl Friedman."

A thousand miles away Sergeant Steffan clears his throat. "What about some other pissed-off student? Besides Raven, I mean."

Images plague Maddy's mind: working late in Stanton Hall, the campus bell tower striking seven, Raven stamping snow from his motorcycle boots.

Is that a picture of your daughter?

Yes.

Better keep an eye on her.

Why, Raven?

I don't know. Just tell her to be careful.

In the outer office a woman sobs hysterically, her frantic words indecipherable to Madelyn, who sits on the edge of the hard chair, close to tears herself.

"Okay," Ben says. "Any others?"

"In each class there are students who feel frustrated or under-appreciated. They tend to blame everyone but themselves—their high schools, their parents, most often their professors. My God, there must have been at least 30 of those over the past fifteen years!"

"I keep thinking about that poem," says Neil Steffan.

"What kind of person would rape a woman, then write a note like that, call her twenty times. Take off on a motorcycle on the spur of the moment—. I'm thinking maybe we're looking for some student druggie with a love/hate thing for women." Maddy and Ben can hear him breathing hard into the mouthpiece. "Know any students who use?"

Madelyn snorts. "Know any students who don't?" Itching for a cigarette, she eyes the rubble of Ben's desk searching in vain for an ashtray.

Ben pulls his chin and stares up at the ceiling fan. "Think about your neighbors. Have you had problems with any of them?"

She shakes her head, lifting her hands palm-up. "Actually, I'm not home all that much, and when I am, I keep pretty much to myself. I'm friendly with Hattie Frankl next door and Gil Everhart one block over. The rest are just nodding acquaintances."

Ben takes rapid notes in a neat script. "How about someone who might be disturbed or burdened by your being here on Cypress Key? Someone who depends on you or your husband for employment, for example. Think, Madelyn."

But she doesn't want to think about such things. What she wants is to reverse time, to recapture the excitement of her arrival, her first walk on the beach.

"The only people I employ are the Home Maids—a bonded housekeeping service that cleans once a month—but they send different workers each time." She stares, unseeing, at a framed photograph of Thomas Jefferson on the wall behind Ben's head. "And then there's Cory Neale, who moonlights as a sort of neighborhood handy man—cuts grass, washes windows, that sort of thing. But he works for others in the neighborhood much more than he does for me." She presses her fingers to her temples. "I've known him for years. He was in my daughter's high school class. Do you mind very much if I smoke?"

Chief Waite takes his time writing on his note pad, then pulls a clean ashtray from his desk drawer and hands it to her. When she can't find her lighter in the jumble of her purse, he tosses her a matchbook, then watches in disapproval as she lights up, inhales deeply, and expels smoke into the room.

Ben removes his glasses and softens his tone. "Forgive me for asking, but could there be a jealous husband somewhere?"

"What do you mean?"

Ben leans forward. "Is it possible your husband is having an affair with someone whose husband wants revenge?"

"David has been out of the country on business since

the middle of September," says Madelyn. "He travels with his assistant, Fatima Kemball—'Tee' for short. He claims they are only business associates."

"But you suspect otherwise?"

"I have wondered from time to time." Madelyn brushes imaginary lint from her denim skirt, choosing her words carefully. "The truth of the matter is, we're separated. David called last week from Amsterdam and suggested we give it another try."

"And you said—"

"That I'd think about it and talk with him when he gets back."

"When will that be?

"I'm not sure. Early January, I think."

Ben leans back in his swivel chair and laces his fingers behind his head. Someone laughs in the hallway, a sound that hangs in the charged air like the smoke from her cigarette.

"What about your daughter Jessica's friends?" asks Neil Steffan. "Any potential troublemakers?"

Despite the stuffiness of Ben Waite's office, Maddy's hands and feet are freezing. She wishes she could crawl beneath Anna Hayes' warm quilt and sleep until this nightmare is over. Instead she grips the arms of her chair to keep from pounding on Ben's desk in impatience.

Of course there are troublemakers! she wants to yell.

Jessie has made a career out of bad boys and ne'er-do-wells! Like the time she deliberately dated that creep Carlos Sanchez after he was hauled into juvenile court for assaulting the high school principal. Or when she thumbed a ride with a Ferris wheel operator, then brought him home to dinner.

"My daughter's in New Mexico," Madelyn says. "She hasn't lived at home for seven months."

The three of them are silent for a moment. Then Neil Steffan speaks slowly, a hint of apology in his tone. "Aside from Victor Manolo, have you perhaps been seeing someone since you and your husband separated?"

Maddy avoids Ben's gaze to mask her mounting hostility. Must she open every detail of her life to public scrutiny? Her voice cuts with a hard edge. "Last March I had cancer surgery. Since then, my health and my career have consumed all my energy." Then in the interest of truth she acquiesces. "In the past two weeks I have resumed my friendship with Adam Devlin, whom I knew years ago at Ohio State."

Ben pushes up from his desk and stands at the window, his long, brown fingers pulling at his chin. In the silence Maddy can hear a telephone ringing hundreds of miles away in Steffan's Ohio precinct and his muffled voice responding to someone's question.

"We're going about this all wrong," Ben says at last. He sits again at his desk and flips to a new page on his legal pad. "If we're going to catch this guy, we have to try to think like he does."

"How can we do that" Maddy asks, "when we don't even know who he is?"

"For starters, by examining the sequence of events in your garage. Tell us again what you remember, Madelyn. Then, Steffan, I'll ask you to fill in the blanks."

She clenches her teeth, draws a deep breath, and begins. "After lunching with Dr. Friedman at the mall, I shopped for a birthday gift for Jessica, then went to a matinee. The movie ended about six. I bought a take-out salad at a deli and drove home in the rain."

Ben holds up one finger to interrupt. "How often do you and Friedman lunch together?"

"Once or twice a semester."

"Any unpleasantness between you?"

Madelyn hesitates. "Only his little game of innuendoes, which makes me uncomfortable. He likes to play kneesies." She shrugs. "I pretend not to notice."

"Have you ever told him to stop?"

"Not in so many words. He's my boss." She watches Ben scribble on his legal pad, feeling powerless and absurd.

"Did you notice anyone in particular sitting near you in the theater?"

"Not many people were there. I sat alone in the back."

"How about in the mall or at the deli? Recall anything out of the ordinary on the part of salespeople or other customers—someone hanging around or appearing to pay undue attention."

"No, no one." He rotates his index finger signaling her to continue.

"It was after 7:30 and very dark when I pulled into my garage. I remember sitting there for a couple of minutes listening to the end of a song on the radio."

"Garage door open or closed?"

"Closed. I always close it before getting out for safety sake. Fat lot of good *that* did!"

"Go on."

"Then I gathered up my parcels and stepped out of the van." Maddy feels her throat constrict and tries to ignore the tension knotting in the pit of her stomach. "He grabbed me from behind with his arm tight around my neck. He told me to get down on the garage floor, which I did. Then he kicked me—hard. I must have blacked out because I don't remember the rest." I will not cry in front of Ben Waite, she thinks. But in spite of her resolve, tears start to spill over.

"Steffen, did anyone check the garage door remote

for a fingerprint?"

"We checked the master remote on the wall, but only read Mrs. Ives' print, so he must have used the portable remote. It was missing from the van when we recovered it."

"What were you wearing?" he asks Madelyn.

"A red raincoat. Skirt and sweater. Black pumps."

"What about him? What did he have on?"

"Dark pants and a vest, one of those quilted, down-filled things. And a black ski mask."

"Don't forget the knife," prompts Steffan.

"Yes, he had a kind of hunting knife, I think, with a blade about six inches long."

"Which hand did he hold it in?"

Maddy frowns in concentration. "Both, I think. First one, then the other."

"You say he spoke to you. What can you tell me about his voice?"

"Gravelly, as if he had a cold. Actually, he kind of whispered."

"Accent?"

"None that I recall." She grimaces. "I could tell he was scared by the way his eyes darted around. And he smelled."

"Of what?"

"A really intense body odor, for starters. And something else. Strong. Maybe vomit?" She wrinkles her nose in disgust.

"You say he kicked you. Do you remember what kind of shoes he had on?"

Maddy shakes her head. "Some kind of heavy boots, I think."

"Like motorcycle boots?"

"I don't remember." A sudden thought occurs. "Vic Manolo wore fancy cowboy boots. If I had seen those, I'm sure I would have recognized them."

"What about gloves? Do you remember gloves?" She looks at him helplessly and shrugs. Ben nods at an idea forming behind his dark, intelligent eyes. "Steffan, your report indicates that he stole her purse, the birthday necklace, and the van."

"And the earring," says Steffan.

"Right, the earring. Give me your perspective on the house."

"On a cul-de-sac," says Steffan. "Large lot, maybe 200 by 300. High hedges between buildings. Several large trees. An attached two-car garage with separate automatic doors. No lights on. Newspaper on the front walk."

Ben is on his feet again, this time pacing around his cluttered office. When Madelyn starts to speak, he holds up a finger, his expression revealing intense concentration.

"Okay, what does all this tells us?" He grabs his pad

and pen from the desk and continues pacing. "It says we've got a guy with the nervous sweats. He's scared, jittery. Why? Maybe because he's a misfit—a punk in a fancy neighborhood."

"Or maybe because he's strung-out on something," offers Steffan. "Cocaine, heroin—"

"Maybe. Anyway, he's deliberately chosen this secluded house, but how did he get there? Not in his own car, which he would have left behind when he drove away in Madelyn's van. Maybe on his motorcycle? Same problem, although I suppose he could have found a way to hide a bike or even load it in the van. Did he take a taxi? No, for obvious reasons."

"It's eighteen blocks to the nearest bus stop," says Steffan.

"He can tell from the newspaper on the front walk and the lack of lights that nobody's home, yet he doesn't break in, take what he wants, and run. He waits in the dark and the rain. Why?"

"Because," says Steffan, "what he wants isn't there. Not yet."

Ben glances over at Maddy, whose pallor belies the determined set of her jaw. "And what does his appearance suggest? He's rough and unkempt. He wears the uniform of a skier or a laborer."

"Or a Lake Erie fisherman," offers Steffan.

SUSAN B. JOHNSON

"Maybe. A sleeveless vest for both warmth and mobility, a cold-weather ski mask, heavy boots."

"Could be steel-toed," says Steffan, "judging from the damage they did."

Ben nods, pausing to jot something on his pad. "He's wearing a mask so she can't I.D. him. He whispers—maybe to disguise his voice? He sexually assaults her *after* she's unconscious as if rape was an afterthought. Seems to me if rape was his primary aim, he'd have come prepared—a rope, a gag, maybe a roll of duct tape. But all he has is his knife."

"The rape kit report indicates no semen, but clearly there was genital contact. So apparently the bastard couldn't perform."

"Could be he blames her for his failure and feels compelled to get revenge, to finish what he started no matter what it takes," says Neil Steffan.

Ben nods slowly. "That may be our motive." He folds his arms and locks eyes with Maddy. "Say I'm a nobody," he begins, "a guy with no friends, no success with women. An angry, ineffectual loser who's been getting the shaft all my life—at home, at school, with women. And I'm desperate to prove myself a man. I fantasize about a pretty, rich woman whom I've been watching for some time, one with enough money to provide me with the power, the prestige, all the drugs I want."

Ben's voice turns menacing. "Then one day something bad happens—I lose my job, or some girl ridicules me—and in a seething rage, my last thread of self-control snaps. I want to strike out, to hurt somebody—an eye for an eye. I plan my revenge, hide my identity, leave no fingerprints. I'm feeling smart, in control, energized."

Ben turns toward Maddy in a half-crouch, his eyes narrowed menacingly. "I wait in the dark for my fantasy woman. I time my attack and take her from behind. Her fear excites me, turns me on. Now *I'm* the powerful one, and I like the feeling, want more, want *her*—"

Maddy closes her eyes and covers her ears. "How can he hate me so much when I don't even know who he is?"

Ben shifts to a gentler tone. "He probably doesn't hate you. As a matter of fact, in some twisted way he may even admire you and want to exert enough control to keep you tied to him in what he views as a relationship." Remember John Hinckley, the man who stalked Jodie Foster and then tried to kill President Reagan to demonstrate his 'love'?"

"But," says Steffan, "at the last minute, this guy can't perform, and this reinforces his rage. He can't dominate her sexually, yet he's obsessed with her. Somehow he finds out where she's going and decides to follow her so he can continue to terrorize her. For him, fear equals power."

"What if none of this is true?" asks Maddy. "How can you proceed on mere speculation?"

Ben stops pacing and leans against his desk. "Just a starting point," he says. "Ever heard of Occam's Razor? It's an old maxim taught in Criminology 101 that says the person with the motive, the means, and the opportunity probably committed the crime." He smiles reassuringly. "So we begin to patch together evidence of someone that fits that profile."

"I say he took the earring for a trophy," says Steffan. "Something he can keep to connect himself to her. Otherwise, why not take both?"

"Good point," says Ben. "He may even decide to wear it himself as a sort of talisman." He makes another note on his yellow pad. Then he stoops beside Madelyn's chair. "Be glad about that ski mask because it probably saved your life. He didn't have to kill you to keep from being recognized. And you're wrong when you say you don't know who he is." He takes her icy hand in his. "You *do* know this man, Madelyn. I'm confident he's someone you've taught or talked to in the supermarket or asked to tune your car. Keep in mind that four out of five rapes are committed by a family member or an acquaintance."

"You've just described Vic," she says.

"Maybe. But not necessarily." He squeezes her fingers. "Which is why, today, I want you to start writing down every idea that comes to you about this whole thing, regardless of how farfetched it seems. The answer is there in your subconscious, which will be working twenty-four hours a day to dredge it up. Agreed?"

He lifts the receiver, excluding Madelyn from the three-way conversation. "That's it for now," he says to Steffan, whose lengthy reply Maddy can't hear. "Right you are, Sergeant. Same drill."

For a moment he scans his notes, then sits in his swivel chair, pushes back, and smiles for the first time. "Good man, that Steffan. Like a terrier with a bone." He nods, narrowing his eyes. "We're gonna get this reptile, Steffan and I. We're gonna nail his ass and ship it off to prison—it's only a matter of time."

Chapter 24

Monday, December 29

With an unsteady hand, Maddy inserts the key into the Miata's door lock, thankful for its lack of space in the rear for an attacker to conceal himself. She slides behind the wheel, exhaling only after both doors are securely locked, and waits for her pulse to subside. This is nuts, she thinks. What can happen in the parking lot of Police Headquarters?

She can't, however, spend the rest of her life here, squeezed between two patrol cars. Where can she go? To some anonymous room at the Harbor Inn? If he can find her on a country road in a rented car, what's to guarantee he can't get to her there? If only Fee hadn't gone to Aruba for New Year's. She checks the rear view mirror, then switches on the ignition, adjusting the heater to warm her freezing feet.

Perhaps she can hide out at Adam's house; she knows he keeps a spare key on a nail beneath the front steps. A prickle of anxiety skitters up the back of her neck. To isolate herself in such a remote place would be foolhardy, an invitation to danger. She'd never have a moment's rest.

Of course she could hop on a Delta flight and be in Cleveland by dinner time. The thought sinks like a stone to the pit of her stomach. Mentally, she enters her house in Willow Park, walks through the cold, vacant rooms. She imagines herself in her old blue robe eating canned soup at the kitchen table, crawling between chilly sheets to sleep alone in the queen-sized bed. No, going back to Belleporte would be just that—going back, regressing to a dying marriage, terrifying memories, and the passive person she no longer wishes to be.

Maddy backs out onto Second Street and resolutely heads south toward Beacon Point Road. She will put her faith in Ben Waite and return to Hayes Cottage, where Boots will be impatient for his kibbles and Adam will soon call to say he's on his way home to spend New Year's Eve with her.

Once past the north end of Lake May, however, her resolve weakens. Even if Ben could promise round-the-clock watch on Hayes Cottage, she wouldn't feel really safe. And she knows he can't spare the manpower, especially given the added burden of dozens of holiday revelers swarming onto the island every day. He has promised to be at her door within five minutes of her call. But five minutes had been plenty of time for her attacker to put a choke hold on her and knock her to the garage floor. More than ever she wishes she had ignored Ben's orders and bought a handgun. Without some means of self-defense, she feels like a balloon on a dart board.

Here and there along the strand, picnickers in jeans and sweaters huddle about charcoal grills or hurl frisbees against the chilly sea breeze. Like tropical birds, windsurfers with purple and aqua sails dip and skim across the Gulf. Madelyn barely notices, so intent is she upon her mirrored view of the road behind her.

She lowers the window six inches to let the fragrant sea breeze calm her ragged nerves, but the sight of a motorcycle parked by the side of the road compels her to close it again. You know this man, she hears Ben say. A clerk in the grocery store. A man from UPS. Think, Madelyn, think.

A mile beyond Hayes Cottage, the paved surface changes abruptly to gravel, causing her purse to overturn and a spiral-bound notebook to jostle to the floor, its open pages revealing doodles, scrawled notes, and lists of names. Someone I've taught, she thinks. Someone I've offended—

like Vic? He fancies himself a poet of sorts, he rides a motorcycle, and God knows he has the potential for violence. Or what about Raven? Or maybe some other angry student?

The thought shakes Madelyn's confidence. In the last eighteen years she has developed the seasoned teacher's ability to diffuse hostilities in the classroom, to side-step sensitive issues and smooth ruffled feathers with humor. And because she encourages her students stretch their minds by playing with ideas, they often use the word "fun" in their end-of-semester evaluations. Three times she has been honored for maintaining the highest student retention rate. Twice she has been nominated as Harding College's Teacher of the Year. To think that she might have overlooked a student so crazed as to rape her, so embittered as to wish her dead, causes her to call into question her own professionalism.

Madelyn turns right into Minneola's rutted dirt drive leading back through the trees. She zigzags to avoid potholes then parks beside a rusted fuel drum near the old woman's shanty. Someone has opened the door to a wire pen allowing a hen and her chicks freedom to peck among the weeds. Once again she is struck by the density of the shade here, the way scrawny saplings yearn upward toward shards of fractured sunlight.

She slips from the car and stands listening, her ear caught by a thin keening of the wind through the pines.

Why have I come? she wonders. Because local lore embraces Minneola as a wise seer and advisor? Not likely. For thirty years she has rejected the metaphysical in preference for the rational. In seventh grade the funeral of Lily Kenner, dead at twelve of heart complications from Down Syndrome, provided Maddy clear evidence of Darwin's survival-of-the-fittest logic. She has, ever since, viewed mankind as an amalgam created from waste, makeshift, and blunder, and regarded belief in the supernatural as a palliative for the intellectually insecure.

No, she has come to this place for neither divine guidance nor voodoo intercession. I am here, she decides, to cut myself some slack and take a break from anxiety. She inhales the perfume of the pine-scented woods surrounding Minneola's shack and rotates her head to release the tension in her neck. So removed is this place from the world of motorcycles and graffiti and conference calls that she is, for the moment, at peace.

When Minneola does not respond to her knock, Madelyn wonders if the old woman has fallen ill or tripped on the uneven floor of her kitchen. She raps again, listening intently for movement within, but Minneola's house sags silently on its crumbling foundation, holding all its secrets within. Worried, Maddy leans close and calls, "Minneola?

It's Madelyn Ives. Are you okay in there?" But the only sound is the whine of the wind in the treetops.

She picks her way between a coil of rusted chicken wire, a broken pail, and a pile of sodden rags to the area behind Minneola's shack, where she finds a fire pit of ashes beneath a black iron kettle, its scummy contents abuzz with flies. Two goats pause to stare at her from beside a weathered outhouse, then lower their heads once again to their grazing.

Maddy looks around for Minneola, then crosses to the back door, which stands ajar. She hesitates, her hand on the knob. *Should I or shouldn't I?*

"Minneola," she calls again. From somewhere within she hears a moan, then silence. She pulls open the door and steps inside, pausing to assess her surroundings in the gloom. This must be the pantry behind the kitchen, Maddy thinks, where she stores her bones and potions. Occupying the full length of a sagging shelf are glass jars of varying sizes, some containing dried vegetation, others full of dark liquid or grayish paste. None are labeled. All are sealed tightly with screw caps or hardened paraffin. Maddy wipes her damp hands on her jeans, feeling out of place and apologetic, a trespasser encroaching on the old woman's privacy.

Enough light filters through the grimy window to

direct Maddy to the kitchen where she finds the table littered with dirty plates and cups. No fresh baked bread aroma today, only a sour, sick-room smell like airless closets and dirty linen. She tiptoes to another door and pauses to listen at the crack, hearing clearly the rales of ragged breathing. Nudging it open, she gasps at the sight before her. On the bed lies Minneola, her eyes open and wild with fever. As she struggles for breath, a terrible rattle sounds in her chest.

"My god, Minneola!" she says, falling to her knees beside the old woman. "Here, let me help you." She pulls a gray blanket up around her shoulders, then rushes to the kitchen for a glass of water, her mind racing. Run to the car. Get to a phone. Call Ben. As she slips her arm beneath the frail shoulders, the old woman begins to flail and thrash, her eyes rolling in her head.

"He coming," she screams. "The black one, he coming!" Her teeth clatter as she struggles against Maddy's grasp, twisting and clawing the air with extraordinary strength. Then as quickly as it began, the seizure ends, and she sinks back upon the pillow, her body laboring for air.

Maddy stands, willing her knees to support her, dabbing at a scratch on her cheek. She is flushed and sweating, shaken by the suddenness of the outburst and the threat that it implies. Who is the "black one?" she wonders. Some demonic product of Minneola's pain and confusion?

Or is he another of her "knowings," for which Maddy is developing a healthy respect?

"Lie quietly," she whispers, stroking the fiery brow. "And don't be frightened. I'm going to go and telephone for help.

Forty minutes later she and Ben Waite watch the Chiefland EMS team load the stretcher and the oxygen tank into the back of the emergency van.

"Where will they take her?" she asks Ben.

"To Shands Hospital in Gainesville. She's in good hands." He gives Maddy's shoulder a squeeze. "Damn fortunate you found her when you did."

She parks the Miata in Anna Hayes' carport and checks the rear view mirror, then collects her purse and heaves herself from the car, almost stepping in Boots' empty water dish. Poor cat. She has forgotten all about him. What a morning! She slips off her shoes in the kitchen, thinking how good a hot bath will feel.

As she starts up the carpeted stairway in her stocking feet, she pauses, her attention caught by the unfamiliar odor of cigar smoke. Where could it be coming from? Her eyes follow the stairs to the top, her ears attentive to any movement, any out-of-the-ordinary noise. A buzz of alarm sounds at the base of her brain as she tries to remember who, if anyone, has been in the cottage since yesterday morning. Not Ben. Not Adam. With growing unease, her mind gropes for an explanation. Could it be coming in from outside? That would mean a window is open somewhere, yet she knows she hasn't opened any since checking the latches last night before going to bed. Had she perhaps left the kitchen door unlocked last evening when she left to pick up Adam at the marina? No, she clearly remembers unlocking it a few moments ago before securing it with the new brass chain.

Madelyn grips the banister with both hands. *Who, besides me, has a key?*

Wynn has one, yet she never said anything about flying to Florida when she called two nights ago. Fee also has a key, but Fee's in the Caribbean.

Perspiration beads her upper lip at the memory of the rapist's acrid smell. Something besides body odor—was it cigars? Once again she sees the knife in his hand, his crazed eyes behind the ski mask. *Geddown!* he had growled. Then he had brought one of his boots to her face.

As she creeps back down the stairs, her knees watery with fright, she hears the echo of Vic's voice: "A good cigar is like a good woman, hot on one end and a tasty mouthful on the other." Vic smokes cigars—dark Brazilians that color the air and make her eyes water.

Maddy's thoughts tumble over each other. This

241

smoke is different somehow—maybe pipe tobacco? Adam sometimes smokes a pipe, and he knows about the spare key hidden in the carport. She glances upward again. But if Adam didn't go to Miami as planned, how did he get here? Neither his truck nor his motorcycle is parked in the drive.

"Adam?" she calls in a half-whisper. "Adam, is that you?"

She tenses, listening for movement but hearing only the thud of her own heart. *Get out now! Go to Ben!* Her eyes skitter about the room looking for any potential weapon—a letter opener, a fireplace poker. Suddenly, upstairs the toilet flushes, the shower starts.

Madelyn deflates on the bottom stair, relief surging through her. Lucky for Adam she didn't call the police! She starts upstairs, chuckling at the image of him standing buck naked, hands above his head, looking down the barrel of Ben's police revolver.

"You gave me quite a start," she says, pushing open the bathroom door. Then she gasps, recoiling. A skinny man with bushy eyebrows and long, black braids stands poised with one foot in the shower and the other on the mat. He grins at her, making no move to cover his nakedness.

"Afternoon," he says, lifting his cigar in salute. With a strangled cry, Madelyn grabs the cordless phone from the bedroom, vaults down the stairs two at a time, and lunges out the front door.

"Hi, Mom," says Jessica. She sits on the front deck in Madelyn's new robe, towel-drying her hair, which spikes up in all directions.

"Run!" yells Madelyn, her eyes wild. "There's a rapist in the house!"

Jessie laughs. "He's not a rapist, Mom. That's just Sidney. He's with me."

Madelyn stares at her daughter. "Sidney who?"

"Lame Horse. He's a Navajo." She wraps the towel around her head like a turban, then stands up, clutching the robe's lapels. "We're on our way to Daytona Beach for New Year's and decided to pop in and say hello." She looks warily at her mother.

Madelyn drops onto a deck chair and struggles to contain her roiling emotions. How dare you scare me like that, she wants to yell. What gives you the right to burst unannounced into my life? But this is Jessica, her beautiful black-haired daughter in whose defiant eyes she sees a needful pleading.

When she can trust herself to speak, she enfolds the girl in an apologetic hug. "How did you find me, and how did you manage to get in?"

"I tried to call you at home, but I kept getting the answering machine, so I phoned Aunt Wynn. Jeez, it was

243

like pulling teeth to get her to tell me where you were. Then when we got here and you weren't home, I called her again. She finally told me about the key in the carport. It was really weird, like she thought I was going to steal something." She pulls the towel from her head and runs her fingers through her short, dark curls. "Boy, after three nights in a sleeping bag, a hot shower sure felt good."

"Where is your car?"

Jessica lifts her chin to her mother. "We're not traveling by car, Mother. We're riding Sidney's motorcycle."

Madelyn's startled eyes rivet on her daughter's face. "You're doing what!

"Don't be such an alarmist. His Yamaha is a great bike, very safe and fuel efficient. We left it over at the local garage getting the drive chain repaired or something. Then we hitched a ride over here. What is that ugly thing you're wearing on your wrist? And why is there a camera on a tripod in the kitchen?"

But Madelyn's mind is in overdrive, flashing on images, trying to separate supposition from truth. It's someone you recognize, Ben had said, someone you have known, talked to, taught. On the other hand, maybe not.

Madelyn crouches beside her daughter's chair and lowers her voice. "Jessie, how long have you known that man upstairs?"

"Why?"

"Just answer me." She presses her fingers against her temples. "Please, I have to know."

"About six months. Oh, God, Mother, this isn't the start of one of your lectures, is it? Because I—"

"When did you leave New Mexico?"

"A week before Christmas. Sidney met my plane in West Virginia."

"Where was he before that?"

"What difference does it make? Why are you grilling me about Sidney?"

Madelyn speaks through clenched teeth. "Answer me. It's important."

Jessie rolls her eyes. "He was at a biker's meet in Charleston, West Virginia." She lifts both palms in a shrug. "That's what he does."

Madelyn rises, still holding the cordless phone. If she could somehow get a look at Sidney's wallet, see if he has her Texaco card—

"I could use some coffee," she says. "How about you? I'll make a pot while you stay right here and enjoy the view."

The shower is still running as she mounts the stairs, her legs rubbery with anticipation. In her brief glimpse of the man, she noticed only his nakedness and his braid—not a lot of information for Ben if he asks her for a description. She listens for a moment at the bathroom door, then tiptoes into her bedroom where, as she has hoped, she finds a jumble of discarded clothing heaped on Anna Hayes' slipper chair. But except for a grimy tee shirt and a pair of men's heavy socks, all the items belong to Jess: size eight jeans, a cotton sweater, bra and panties. He has taken his trousers—and his wallet—into the bathroom.

A moment of disappointment gives way to a new idea. Keeping one eye on the bathroom door, she dials Ben's number, praying against hope that he'll be there.

"C'mon, Ben," she whispers, dancing with nervousness.

"Police headquarters," says a woman's voice. "Officer Wright speaking."

"Paula, this is Madelyn Ives. Something's happened, and I need to speak to the chief right away."

"He's off the island until this afternoon," says Paula. "Can I help you?"

"God, I hope so. My daughter arrived today with a man who just might be—" Suddenly the rush of water stops behind the bathroom door. "Look, I don't have time to explain. Please, just run a license check on a Yamaha motorcycle from New Mexico that was brought in either last night or this morning for repair at one of the local

garages. And ask Ben to call me the minute he gets back."
She scuttles downstairs to the kitchen, conscious of a
twitching in her left eye.

"We're ninety-nine percent sure it's the same bike,"
says Ben. "A black Kawasaki 500 with an Ohio plate."

"A Kawasaki? But what about the Yamaha?" She
whispers into the receiver, glancing around to make sure
Jess and the Indian are out of range. "The one in the repair
shop."

"My man Cade's checking that out. In the meantime,
Paula spotted this kid wearing a helmet with a decal of a
shield just like the one in your photograph. Since he has
neither proof of ownership nor license to drive a
motorcycle, she brought him in for questioning. She's on
her way to pick you up so you can take a look."

"Now?"

"Yes, now, because I can't hold him for long."

*Cold cement floor. Grime on the hem of her red
coat. Move and you're dead!* "Will I have to face him?"

"Trust me, he'll never know you're there."

Twenty minutes later, Maddy fidgets on a chair in a
darkened side room of the police station, her heart
galloping wildly. Beyond the one-way mirror is a similar
room, bare except for a table and four chairs. Absurdly,
someone has taped a Santa poster next to a wall display of

criminal profiles.

She sits on her hands to keep them from shaking. What if she can't identify him? On the other hand, what if she can? Will the next few moments be the climax to this whole terrible episode? She wants to nail this bastard. She wants to bolt. What can be taking Ben so long?

Behind her Paula enters, a clipboard in one hand and a styrofoam cup in the other. "Just take your time," she says, handing Madelyn black coffee. "An officer will seat him so he faces us and will ask him a series of questions. Listen closely to his voice, and be sure to notice his hands, his shoes, his body language." She smiles at Maddy and pats her shoulder. "I know this is tough, but so are you."

The moment the door opens, something leaden plummets to the pit of Maddy's stomach. Before her is a child, a stoop-shouldered, frightened teenager whom she has never seen before in her life. She shakes her head, her eyes welling.

"No," she says, swallowing hard. "He's not the one."

Chapter 25

Tuesday, December 30

Cap leans the old bicycle against the inside wall of the marina's storage shed and looks around for a place to stash the weapon in case Ernie Shaver, the dock master, decides to snoop around.

He pulls a wad of money from his pocket—nine fifties, six twenties, and three tens. Six hundred even. Not too bad for a thirteen-year-old Kawasaki 500 with 91,000 miles, a faulty starter, and two bald tires. He'd rather have the money any day, especially since he found out the bike might be attracting a whole lot of heat. Pure luck he had stopped for a beer and a sandwich at the Hammerhead and overheard some bikers bitching about questions from the police, like how's the weather in Ohio and does your helmet have a shield. *Stupid yahoo cops.*

He got lucky again earlier this afternoon when he

SUSAN B. JOHNSON

found a kid so eager to buy the bike that he didn't even test drive it or ask for a bill of sale. Bought into that bullshit about mailing him the title. Used Rollo Guzman's name in case the cops pick the kid up for driving without a motorcycle license. Dumbass almost shit his pants when he got the helmet for free.

He shoves the wad and the weapon deep inside his sleeping bag, reminding himself to slip Ernie Shaver a few bucks for letting him bunk here in the shed. The rest of the cash, if he's careful, will keep him in food and crank for a couple of weeks at least. He can tell Shaver doesn't deal, but that's okay. Now that he's tight with Elva Pastan over at Papa Pépé's, she'll get him whatever he wants.

Cap watches dust swirl in a shaft of late afternoon sunlight and sweeps the plains of his mind for the first stirring of the locusts. No larval quiver beneath the surface, no tremble of wings. So far so good.

In his terror, he had once told Velma Cady, the cook, about the locusts, about how their whirring swells inside his head until it floats up and up, bearing his body away into blackness. Emissaries of the Holy Ghost, she warned, holding him tightly against her bony chest. Fear forced him to endure her probing fingers, the smell of onions and old flesh. Yet even when Velma Cady removed her false teeth and took him into the wet, pink O of her

250

mouth, the locusts would come anyway, would deposit their sticky carapaces in his brain and then ooze away into temporary torpor. By force of will, he steadies his breathing and shakes the memory away.

Instead, Cap thinks about Madelyn Ives, how she had spun away from him with her eyes all wild and hot. He'd had to slap her around a little to keep her quiet, but how'd he know she was gonna just lay there like roadkill? No wonder he hadn't gotten off. Bitch owes him for that. *Treats me like I'm crazy or stupid. Well, we'll just see about that, Mama. We'll just see about that.*

Stretching out on the camp cot, he checks the beams overhead. Coils of wire rope. Anchor line. Oars of various lengths. Shaver was okay about him fixing up the old three-speed in the corner. A new chain was all it needed. Instant transportation! Meantime, he'll make himself useful around the marina. Pump diesel. Run the hoist if they'll let him. Best way to get the keys to Shaver's truck.

He scratches beneath his chin where the new growth still itches. *Beard coming in good. Pretty soon even Joystick won't recognize me.*

Cap stretches, then strips down to his shorts, swiping at his armpits with his sweaty tee-shirt. Just cool it for one more day. One more until he gets what he's come for. He grins in the dim light of the shed as he pulls on Ernie's old oil-stained jumpsuit and rolls up the pant legs.

Five minutes later he is scrubbing down the decks of *Honey Pot* with a scrub brush and a bucket of sudsing ammonia. He braces for the sting as the sun-peeled backs of his hands plunge into the strong detergent, winces as the bony plates of his knees grind against the fiberglass. *Always on my fucking knees. First to oblige Mama, then Booger Mendel, then Sister Henry, and now Ernie Shaver.*

He sits back on his heels and draws a sleeve across his forehead, looking upward at the club pennant flying from the yacht's bow flagstaff. *Get me one of these babies someday.* He feels the old rage beginning its slow crawl upward from the base of his gut. *Get me a big house like hers. Get me a 60-inch plasma TV and a silver Cadillac Escalade.*

He fingers the diamond in his earlobe, still tender from recent piercing. Not even three weeks since he had knelt beside her and sliced away what was his. He scrubs hard at a rust stain near the scupper.

Cap hums to himself, shutting out the whine of the hoist and the jingle of halyards. He'd do her tomorrow night, New Year's Eve, a time for resolutions. He smiles to himself and directs his mind inward to the place where the locusts lie dormant, the rage seethes, and the final plan begins to take shape.

Chapter 26
Tuesday, December 30

Dark eyes. Maybe blue. Maybe brown I can't say. I am five-eight in my black pumps, so he was about five-eleven. Not quite as tall as David. Hard to estimate his weight, but more than David, more than 170 lbs. Rough hands. Callused, like a farmer or a builder. Or a grave digger! Solid build like Vic—maybe a construction worker? or a Marine? Why did I write "Marine"? Did something about him suggest the military?

Frustrated, Maddy caps her pen and clips it to the cover of the journal. Why, on a quick trek through the supermarket, does her photographer's eye register an endless catalog of images that she can later remember in detail—water droplets on ripe tomatoes, a regiment of soup cans, liver slick with congealing blood—yet during significant life events, her senses betray her. When she thinks of her wedding, for instance, she has no memory of the flower-filled church or of David in his tuxedo, only of a tree branch in silhouette beyond a stained-glass window. She recalls nothing of her college graduation except the uneven floor of the stage. And when she thinks of Jessica's birth, she remembers the burn scars on the hands of the pediatric nurse.

In the room with the sloping ceiling, Maddy turns out the light and stretches the length of Anna Hayes' bed, forcing herself to accept its warmth. Two weeks ago she slept here in complete trust, an Eden of safety. Then came the lunatic on a motorcycle. She waits, tensed, for the tinkle of broken glass, for the creak of the top stair, for his breathing at her bedroom door.

"The black one, he coming!" Minneola had screamed in her delirium. But at least for now, all Maddy hears is the hum of the refrigerator and the soft bong of the grandfather clock striking ten in the hall.

She turns onto her side and draws up her knees, part of her glad for the return of privacy, another part terrified of solitude. If only Adam were here. Or Ben. Or even David. Why must she always depend on men to make her feel safe?

"Oh, I forgot to tell you," Jessie had said during today's lunch. "Some man called while you were at the grocery store. I made a note on the pad by the phone."

Maddy had paused, a forkful of chicken salad halfway to her mouth, while across the table her uninvited house guest helped himself to another piece of garlic bread. For some reason she found it impossible to call him "Sidney," and since "Lame Horse" was out of the question, she had managed to be cordial without addressing him at all.

He had spent most of the morning with the hatchet, splitting kindling for Maddy's fireplace and stacking it neatly on the deck beside the kitchen door. Like Adam, he respected good tools and had whetted it to a razor sharp edge, demonstrating its effectiveness by cutting off a few strands of Jessica's hair. Watching him made Maddy queasy with anxiety. At the same time, a flood of memories transported her back to Falter Farm more than twenty years before.

It's all in the wrist, Mad. Throwing a hand axe is like writing poetry. It takes on its own rhythm. Hold the hatchet lightly, like this. Think of it as an extension of your arm. When the moment is right, loft it overhand in one clean movement, never taking your eye off target.

When she could sink the blade four out of five times, Adam had rewarded her with a hatchet of her own that he found at a flea market. Then he showed her how to hone it properly, using a file, a whetstone, and a drop of motor oil. What had become of that hatchet, she wondered, or of all the years since then?

Through a gap in the kitchen curtain, Maddy had measured the breadth of Sidney's shoulders, trying to picture them clad in a down-filled vest. With knotted stomach she watched his powerful forearm flex and release, saw the weapon bite deeply into the end of a log, heard him pound the coupled hatchet and wood onto the ground until a clean split released the blade, ready for the next blow.

She shuddered inwardly, reminded of the look on Vic's face last October when she had hurled the hatchet at the sycamore to stop his mockery. She thought, Jessie and I share an attraction for dangerous men.

"Did he leave a message?"

"Just a telephone number. And his name. Adam something." The change in Maddy's expression was not lost on Jessica. "He seemed surprised when I said I was your daughter. Who is he?"

Now is not the time, Maddy answered silently. Someday, my darling girl, you and I will talk frankly about Adam Devlin. But not until you get your life together. And certainly not in front of what's-his-name. "A friend of a friend," she replied, hating herself.

Ben had called at four, his voice froggy with fatigue, his news disappointing. "The bike in the shop is registered in New Mexico to a Sidney L. Horse. Brought in yesterday for a replacement drive chain. Horse was ticketed for speeding in Denton, Texas, three weeks ago; otherwise, he's clean. You know this Sidney Horse?"

Later, feeling apologetic, she had tucked $50 into Jessica's pocket, packed fruit and sandwiches, and waved them on their way, her beautiful daughter astride the Yamaha behind the man with the long, black braids.

Then she had punched in the number written on the telephone pad. To her dismay, she was connected to room 416 at Mt. Sinai Hospital in Miami. Adam picked up on the second ring.

"Adam! What's happened?"

"Fucking Florida drivers," he said, sounding groggy. "I was part way into an intersection waiting to make a left turn, and some old guy rear-ended me hard and sent me into oncoming traffic. A woman in a new Audi was accelerating to make the light and smashed into me. Fortunately, she and her kid are okay, but all three vehicles are a mess."

"What about you?"

He sighs. "Me—I have a fractured right ankle that's going to need at least one pin They've scheduled me for surgery at 8:30 tomorrow morning. The hell of it is I'll be spending tomorrow night here in the hospital instead of celebrating New Year's with you. You have no concept of how that pisses me off."

Madelyn eased her grip on the receiver. "How long will you be in a cast?"

"Six to eight weeks at least. Then on crutches for another month. Guess I won't be launching *Osprey* until spring." She heard him sigh. "I'm really sorry about this, Mad, but at least you've got your daughter there to keep you company."

Wrong! She wanted to yell. *She's gone, Fee's gone, everybody's gone, I'm all alone!*

"I'll be fine. It's you I'm worried about."

"Hold on," he said, covering the mouthpiece. She heard him speak with someone but couldn't make out his words. After a moment, he returned. "I've got to go," he said. "They need to run some tests."

Maddy had made a sudden decision. "I'm coming to Miami. I'll leave here immediately and be there when you come out of the anesthetic."

Adam's answer came quickly. "No, don't. Enjoy the time with Jessica, and I'll be home in a few days."

"But you'll need help."

She sensed a brief moment of hesitation, no more than for an indrawn breath, but long enough to put her on her guard.

"I'll have help," he said. "Jo Patton's here. Remember meeting her the night of Fee's party? She owns a house out on the beach where I can hang out for a day or two. Then she'll drive me back to the island."

Maddy felt something small and brittle shatter inside. "I see," she had said. Which was a lie. She remembers the casual way Adam slipped an arm around Jo at Fee's party and wishes she weren't so reckless with her own heart.

Suddenly a flash of memory forces her upright in bed—the smell of the man in the garage. Sweat. Vomit. And something else acrid and offensive, but what? She reaches for the light switch and her journal. *Nothing so ordinary as cigars, yet familiar all the same. Rotten meat?*

She feels again the strength of him as he pins her against his body, a knife in his left hand, his right arm crooked around her throat.

His sleeve, striped with mucus and smelling of— of— What? Something disgusting. Urine?

Closing her eyes, she casts her thoughts back to the strong smells of girlhood: Formaldehyde in Mr. Corelli's biology lab. A mixture of cabbage and Lysol in the dining hall at O.S.U. The litter box in Aunt Olivia's pantry where Miss Pretty did her business. And suddenly she has it: *Manure!*

Maddy stares at the word she has written in her journal, her mind roiling with images. She sees sunlight filtering through the dirty panes of Adam's dairy barn studio, smells the perfume of turpentine and wet clay and Phil LaMotte's Gauloise cigarettes. Phil had little to say as he sat atop a ladder, palate in hand, squinting at his work through thick yellow lenses. Gigantic oil paintings— demonic red shapes writhing on a sea of black.

The next two stalls contained the work of Niles Nathan, whose delicate copper wire sculptures earned him, in equal measure, respect from the art community and scorn from his Wall Street father.

A flushing trough ran the length of the barn, separating the two male artists from Jenny Finney, whose potter's wheel hummed and squeaked as she turned out pot after pot, each nearly identical to the one before.

Adam worked in the end stall amid chips and wood shavings, his chisels organized according to length on a burlap-covered bench.

On cold afternoons, she would pull an old cushion to a sunny corner of the dairy barn and study, enjoying the rich aromas, his company, and Dub-the-raccoon curled at her side. Later when the light began to fail, she and Adam would tramp across the fields, holding hands and talking about art or books or the foreign film at the local cinema.

One particular afternoon in late spring she had arrived at Falter Farm to find the studio deserted, all four artists driven away by the eye-watering stench of pig manure spread that morning on the adjacent field. Never before had she smelled anything so vile, and never since— until that night in her garage when the rapist held his arm across her throat.

"Geddown!" he had hissed.

And in the dark of Hayes Cottage, Maddy obeys, sliding beneath the blanket, clutching the pillow to her breast.

She pulls on her red raincoat, disturbed to find one button missing, another dangling from a thread. *Can't meet Adam like this.* On her hands and knees she gropes for a sewing box in the pitch black of Anna Hayes' walk-in closet, suddenly aware that both knees are torn and sticky with blood. *Maybe there's a first aid kit in here somewhere.* As she reaches into a dark corner, she touches something pointed and sharp—a dagger perhaps, or the tip of a sword. Gingerly, her fingers explore its length, coming to rest on a human hand, warm and callused and alive. She recoils in horror, scrambling backward like a crab to the place where the closet door should be, but now she finds only a wall. The air fouls with something fetid, something she remembers from before, and she starts to gasp for breath, her fingers clawing at the plaster. *Gotta get out. Gotta get air. The black one, he coming!*

An animal cry wrenches her back from dreams, and she scrambles, sweating and trembling, from her jumble of covers. She sits rigidly on the edge of Anna Hayes' bed, testing the sound in the echo chamber of her mind. The scream of a gull? Squalling cats? The night is black and still as her icy feet grope for her slippers. She pockets Anna Hayes' letter opener and moves toward the carpeted stairs, pausing at the top to measure the silence. Over the jackhammer of her heart, she hears muted surf sounds, the drip-drip of the bathroom faucet, a familiar creak as she shifts her weight onto the second step.

"Who's there?" Maddy calls in a strangled whisper. Gripping the dagger's ivory handle, she begins her descent, every hair on her head a sentinel to danger.

I'm going crazy, she thinks. I'm hearing things. What must Sidney Lame Horse have thought of her wary expression, her rigid cordiality? Even Jessica had noticed.

"Lighten up, Mom. He's an Indian, not a space alien!"

Tensely, she tours the lower rooms, switching on lamps as she goes, checking security chains, dead-bolts, locks on the ground floor windows. All normal, all secure, their familiarity mocking her fear. There are her sandy

Reeboks on the mat beside the kitchen door. On the table lies her unfinished letter to David.

"Dear David," it begins. "Since your last telephone call, I have done a lot of thinking and have come to several conclusions. First—"

The clock on the stove reads 11:30 p.m. Eight hours until the sun rises. Eight-and-a-half until Ben is at his desk, until she can tell him about the manure smell on the rapist's sleeve. She will start calling at 7:45 in case he gets in early.

Maddy bites down hard on her lower lip, determined to endure. What she will *not* tell Ben is how much she wishes she had never come to this isolated place. What she will *not* allow herself to do is cry.

She fills Boots' bowl with kibbles, then turns on the gas beneath the teakettle and sits down to wait, clutching her robe at her throat. Suppose he's out there, the man with the pig smell. What if he's waiting in the carport, his eyes glittering through the holes in the black ski mask, his long knife poised—

She stares at the row of knives gripped by the magnetic holder beside the kitchen sink: a heavy cleaver for chopping, a serrated bread slicer, and a series of parers with sharp edges and pointed tips. Draping a dish towel over the blades, she lights a cigarette and then begins to pace, checking the location of other potential weapons: a heavy iron skillet on a hook beside the stove, a small crock of black pepper next to the flour canister, a two-pronged grilling fork in the drawer beneath the toaster.

From the top shelf in the pantry, she collects a large pipe wrench and a staple gun, stashing them beneath the kitchen sink. In the living room she notes the hatchet and the poker, both propped beside the fireplace.

At the scream of the teakettle, she whirls, nearly overturning a lamp. Her mind reels. *This is a war zone. I am under siege.*

By 11:45 she has changed her mind about calling Ben, deciding instead to be at the police station when he gets there in the morning, to tell him face to face. It is clear to her that the man she photographed from Fee's balcony—the one who wore his watch on his right wrist—is the same man who held her with his right arm, brandishing the knife in his left. Chilled, she grabs an old black cardigan from a hook beside the door, but as she starts to pull it on over her pajamas, she freezes in mid-motion: the man in the photograph had dressed entirely in black—black pants, black tee-shirt, black helmet!

"The black one, he coming!"

Maddy clutches the door jamb for support. Minneola had known. Even in her delirium, the old woman had tried to warn her!

She reaches for the telephone to call Ben at home,

then changes her mind. What, after all, does she have to report? That she can't sleep? That she hears strange noises? An announcement about pig manure hardly justifies rousing him from sleep.

What about Wynn? She's a night person—she'll still be up. Maddy grabs the phone and punches in the number. Wynn's sleepy voice answers on the second ring.

"Greenscape."

"Wynn, it's me. Were you asleep?"

"What the hell time is it?"

"About midnight. Listen—"

"Are you okay? You sound strange."

"Wynn, talk to me about pig manure."

A rustling sound occupies the long pause on the other end of the line. Maddy pictures her friend turning on the bedside light, frowning at the clock, punching up her pillows to sit upright in the bed. "Madelyn, have you been drinking?"

"C'mon, I really need to know. Tell me who uses it and for what."

Her friend clears her throat, summoning a tolerant tone. "Practically nobody. Sometimes it's used for soybeans. I recently got some from a hog farmer over in Deever who lets me pay in trade. What in hell is going on there?"

"You use pig manure?"

"Once in a while. It's rich in nutrients, good for replenishing fallow soil. Of course it smells like, well, pig manure, which a lot of people find offensive." She yawns. "Why are we having this bizarre conversation in the middle of the goddamn night?"

Maddy drums her fingers against the receiver, then plunges ahead. "Because I'm sure the man who raped me had pig shit on his sleeve. It's a smell you don't forget." She underlines "soybeans" on the telephone pad. "Now all I have to do is find a pig farmer who rides a motorcycle, and I can nail the sonofabitch."

Chapter 27
Wednesday, December 31

Ordinarily, Maddy wouldn't have heard it—the quiet footfall on the back deck. Two quick steps, then silence as if someone were listening at the kitchen door. But apprehension has sensitized her, enabling her to hear beneath the ordinary sounds of life, like the safe cracker she once read about who sanded his fingertips to heighten his sense of touch. Maddy holds her breath, waiting for another sound, knowing with a visceral certainty that this night will change her life forever.

She perches, tensed and motionless, on the edge of the easy chair that she has dragged to the corner near the kitchen door, daring only to slide her eyes to the luminous dial of her watch. Twenty-five past twelve, only thirty minutes since her phone call to Wynn.

On rubbery legs, she edges to the kitchen bay, careful to avoid the booby-trap of stacked drinking glasses ready to tumble should anyone push open the door. Her finger locates the shutter button of her Pentax still aimed through the gap in the curtains toward the back deck. *Maybe the flash will scare him away.* When she looks through the lens, she sees only a hanging begonia and below it on the porch railing an old pair of rubber thongs.

She waits for her thumping heartbeat to subside, then returns to her chair, a meat cleaver tucked beside her and the upstairs cordless phone in her lap.

She feels like a child again—little Madelyn, terrified of the dark, insisting that the hall light remain on, the bedroom door ajar. Daddy had sympathized, rubbing her back and humming lullabies until she was too sleepy to protest his leaving. But Rose resolutely snapped off the light, stating that such fears were the purview of children less gifted and rational. Madelyn, she reminded the child, was a McCandless, in whom such nonsense would not be indulged.

A scratching noise like fingernails against the kitchen door brings her to her feet, her back rigid, every hair a sensor. Her ears ring with the strain of concentration.

When she hears a key turning in the lock, she moves to a half-crouch behind the chair and picks out Ben's home number on the illuminated dial. *Be there, Ben,* she prays. Terrified, she watches the door ease open as far as the chain will allow.

"Mom?" calls a voice through the crack. "It's me, Jess. Can you let me in?"

Maddy nearly collapses in relief. She sits on the floor with eyes closed, one hand clutching her stomach, the other across her mouth to keep from bursting into tears. Finally, she gathers herself to her feet, shoves aside the tower of drinking glasses, and opens the door.

"I tried not to wake you," Jessica says, pushing past her, "but I forgot about the safety chain. Do you know your little red car has a flat?" She lays the spare key on the table and switches on the kitchen light. "What's wrong? You look as if you've seen a ghost."

"It's just that I thought you and—and—"

"Sidney, mother." She sighs elaborately. "We had a fight. He took off."

"You mean he left you?"

"In a truck stop just north of Ocala." She slumps onto a kitchen chair and bites down hard on her lower lip. "We were going to go to this all-night biker blast out on Daytona beach with lots of free food and beer and a band, you know? Everybody was going to be there. And then at exactly midnight—." Her eyes fill, and she swallows hard. "This would have been our first New Year's Eve together."

"How did you get back?"

"Hitched with a trucker as far as Gainesville, then

SUSAN B. JOHNSON

caught a ride with some kids to the island. They let me off down the beach, and I walked the rest of the way."

Madelyn studies her daughter. Something about her has changed—a weariness perhaps, a hard edge softened. "Why are you still wearing dark glasses at midnight?"

Jessica deflates like a pool toy. She averts her face for a moment, then slowly removes her sunglasses and turns to face her mother, who gasps at the puffy, discolored flesh, the gash above the lid still oozing blood beneath its sodden Band-Aid.

"My God, Jessie. He did this to you?"

"It looks worse than it feels."

Madelyn struggles to contain her rage. I'll kill the sonofabitch myself, she thinks, rummaging in the medicine cabinet for Q-tips, alcohol, gauze, and adhesive. When she returns to the kitchen, she sees that Jessica has pulled free the soiled bandage causing the wound to bleed anew.

"Honey, you should have a stitch."

"Can't you just butterfly it closed?"

"I'll do my best, but I really think—" Carefully she wipes around the cut with a moist wash cloth. "Brace yourself," she says, dipping a swab in the alcohol. "This is going to sting."

Once, thinks Madelyn, you would have screamed at me for hurting you like this. Once you would have stomped

270

out of the house, full of rage and indignation. Who is this passive, trusting girl offering up her face to me, and where is my feisty Jessica?

As she leans close to inspect her work, she feels Jessie's arms creep about her waist and a warm cheek press against her stomach. "I love him, Mom," Jessie says, her voice wobbly. "I don't know what I'm going to do."

Moved more by the gesture than by the words, Madelyn closes her eyes. She can't remember the last time she felt her daughter's embrace. After a moment, Jessie releases her with her a wan smile.

"Can I make you a sandwich?" Maddy asks.

"I'm too tired to eat. If you don't mind, I'll just crash in the downstairs bedroom."

Suddenly a wash of fear floods Madelyn. "You can't stay here," she says.

Jessica's face crumples with hurt and disappointment. "Sidney won't come here, if that's what you're thinking. He's probably on the beach partying it up with some other girl by now." She presses both hands against her mouth and begins to cry.

Madelyn kneels beside her daughter's chair. "No, that's not what I meant," she says, stroking the girl's silky head. She draws a huge breath and plunges ahead. "Jessica, look at me for a moment. The last thing in the world I want to do is send you away. But I think it would be better if you

271

didn't spend the night here."

The girl's dark eyes grow even darker. "Why? What's going on?"

Madelyn rises and begins to pace, searching for the right way to say what she feels she must. "I don't want to frighten you," she begins, "but for several weeks, someone has been harassing me. The police are trying to establish his identity, but at this point we still don't know who he is."

"What do you mean by 'harassing?' What exactly does he do?"

"At home he would call ten or twenty times every night. Then when I arrived here—"

"Are you saying some creep followed you here all the way from Ohio?"

"We're not really sure. But we think he rides a motorcycle."

"God almighty," Jessica says. "Now I understand about the camera aimed out the window and why you acted so weird around Sidney."

"I'm sorry about that. But I have to be so careful."

Jessie nods. "So tell me the rest."

And despite herself Maddy does just that—a headlong plunge into the rape in the garage, the threatening note, the Texaco charges, the photographs, the graffiti, even the part about Minneola. Jessica's face pales as she listens, making her purple eye appear even more ghoulish. By the time Maddy finishes, the girl is trembling with outrage.

"Men are such *shits!*" she yells. "Where the hell is Dad? Why isn't he here?"

"I didn't tell him. He doesn't need to know."

"Why the hell not?"

Here it is, thinks Maddy. The perfect opening. *Because*, she can imagine herself saying, *while you've been living in New Mexico, David and I have not managed one truthful discussion, one night of intimacy, even one good belly laugh. He clearly prefers his double-breasted business associate, Tee Kemble. And I have fallen hard for Adam Devlin, who—*. "He's in Europe on business," she says. "What could he possibly do?"

"I don't know, get you out of here, take you someplace safe."

But Maddy dismisses the idea with a wave. "Jessie, you may find this hard to believe, but I'm beyond needing your father to solve my problems. *Way* beyond." She resumes her pacing, the gears of her mind a whirr. "Some friends of mine, the Jacobys, run a hotel here on the island." She glances at her watch and frowns. "It doesn't matter that it's late. I'm going to give them a call, see if I can get you a room, have them send a car for you."

"You come with me."

For a moment, Madelyn hesitates, then tightens her

resolve. *Whatever happens, it happens to me, not Jessica. If she's with me, she's as much a target as I am.*

"No, I need to stay. I can't let this madman run my life. But the police are patrolling the neighborhood, keeping close watch." She hopes to God this is true.

"Then I'm staying too," says Jessica. She lowers her head onto her arms and begins to sob.

Madelyn kneels beside her, smoothing the soft, black curls. She wraps her arms around her, thinking of the countless times she has stood by, trying by force of will to absorb her daughter's distress. On the ride to the hospital, for instance, after Jessie's fall from the Grunwald's apple tree, Madelyn had steadied the child's fractured arm and crooned the same words she whispers now: "Sh-h-h, I know you're hurting, but tomorrow you'll feel better."

After a few moments, Jessica lifts her head and wipes her eyes on her sleeve.

"I'm so tired," she mumbles. "I haven't had a really good night's sleep in—I can't even remember. Please don't make me leave." Like an old woman, she slumps in her chair, her shoulders rounded in fatigue.

Madelyn wavers, torn between sympathy and protectiveness. Finally, her heart wins out. From the powder room she fetches two white tablets and a tumbler of water. "Swallow these. They'll help you to sleep soundly."

Jessica obeys. Then, supported by her mother, she half-stumbles to the tiny first-floor bedroom where Madelyn helps her out of dusty jeans and into a clean cotton nightgown. By the time she draws the covers over her and turns off the bedside lamp, the girl is snoring softly.

Madelyn hangs Jessie's jean jacket on a peg behind the door, then tosses her dirty tee shirt and underwear into the washing machine. She adds detergent and bleach as the water rises, taking satisfaction from being in control of at least this one small part of her life. Despite her weariness she senses a new strength building within her, a steel-banded determination to protect herself and Jessica from the malevolence of her tormentor. *He's not going to win,* she vows, snapping off the kitchen light, *because I'm not going to let him.*

She draws aside the curtain and stands in the dark, listening to the pound of distant surf and gazing out across the back deck to the sea grass curtseying in the gulf breeze. When the grandfather clock strikes two, she starts upstairs, her feet leaden, her head thrumming with fatigue.

At 2:40 a. m. the telephone rings, shattering the silence. Immediately awake, Madelyn grabs the receiver and brings it to her ear, hearing rapid breathing, a light tap-tapping at the other end of the line. Oddly, the sound calms her, giving her a direction, a strength of purpose. She draws a breath and yells into the telephone:

"Stop calling me!"

But it's Wynn's voice she hears from eight-hundred miles away. "Madelyn, it's gotta be him! It's got to be Cory. I've been such a bloody idiot!"

"What!"

"Cory Neale, my yard foreman! Everything fits, don't you see? We were in the middle of spreading hog manure on that new acreage where I'm starting a Christmas tree farm, and Cory was in charge. Then halfway through the project, he just disappeared. He talked me into giving him his check a day early, and he drove away. On his motorcycle! I haven't heard from him since!"

Madelyn's chaotic thoughts tumble over one another. "Cory Neale? But he practically lived at our house when he was a kid. He had this thing for Jessica, but she—"

"Well, he's not a kid any more. Jesus, have you seen him lately? Powerful arms and shoulders. Hands like hams. What day did you fly to Florida?"

Maddy shakes her head in effort to remember. "Uh, Wednesday, I think. December seventeenth."

Despite Wynn's best effort at self-control, her voice trembles with fury. "Listen, Mad, I've thought for several months there's something creepy about Cory, like maybe he's nuts or on drugs or something. I don't trust his mood swings, for one thing. He's either erratic and hostile or totally mellowed out. And more than once I've suspected him of dipping into the till."

Maddy presses her fingers into her pounding temples. She *has* seen Cory Neale recently. On the way home from the hospital, she had waited in the truck while Wynn stopped to check out a job with one of her workmen. She had not known Cory from the back as the two of them conversed; only when he turned in profile did she recognize the jutting nose and chin of the teenager she had befriended. Is such a thing possible? Can a man commit an act of terrible violence one day, then blithely rake leaves the next? Madelyn feels herself growing lightheaded, her world turning turtle.

Not only that, she had watched Cory Neale replace her burned-out floodlight *later that same day!* Maddy licks her dry lips. "Is he left-handed?" she asks.

"Yes," Wynn squeals. "Oh my God, I just realized something. Remember I told you David telephoned from Amsterdam the night you left? Well, Cory took the call and brought the phone out to the potting shed. He must have hung around listening to me tell David where to find you!" She is crying now and pounding on her bed table and shouting into Maddy's ear. "Mad, you've got to get out of there. Right now, do you hear me? Don't—"

And then the line goes dead.

Chapter 28
Wednesday, December 31

Maddy stares at the dead cordless phone, stunned by the knowledge that time has run out. Wynn's words carom off the corners of her mind. *Cory Neale—the geeky kid from Hope House. That just can't be! I was kind to him. I fed him and gave him odd jobs so he'd have a little spending money! Why, of all people, would he want to hurt me?*

Fragmented images: Cory stacking firewood in David's cast-off lumber jacket; Cory angry and near tears from Jessica's taunting; Cory stuffing Maddy's *Oxford Book of English Verse* into his book bag. She had been pleased to lend it to him, annoyed when he didn't bring it back.

Of course, Coleridge! The source of the threatening poem! Another piece of the puzzle falls into place.

Sickened, she sees herself emerging from the shower wrapped in a towel, remembers the shock of seeing sixteen-year-old Cory perched on the edge of the bed. Even back then she had sensed in his look something unhealthy, almost predatory. From that day forward he was no longer invited into the house.

Two years later the Army made a man of him. Or maybe not. Hadn't Jessica once told her that Cory received a Section Eight discharge? Didn't that mean the Army thought him mentally unstable? Was that why she wrote "marine" in her journal, a subconscious memory of heavy boots, military issue?

She begins to shake as one by one the images return: Calling her friend from the hospital. Waiting in Greenscape's truck while Wynn checked out a job. Noticing with surprise the breadth of Cory's shoulders, the powerful cords in his neck and arms. Later watching through the window as he fixed her security light. My God, he had stood on a ladder less than twenty feet away. How could she not have recognized the man who had nearly killed her just forty-eight hours earlier?

Grabbing the flashlight from beside the bed, Maddy scrambles to her feet. In mounting panic, she steps over the tripwire at the top of the stairs and hurries down to the kitchen in the dark. *Got to rouse Jessica, to warn her. Got to arm us both. The hatchet. The cleaver.*

She reaches for the light switch, then jerks back her hand as if burned. *No lights! He could be right outside!* In her haste she nearly upends her tripod. *The black one, he coming!*

Maddy drops to her knees and rummages beneath the kitchen sink, mentally cataloging spray cleaner, Lysol, insecticide—each a potential weapon. *Stay in control. Get to Jessica.*

As she hurries across the kitchen, her bare foot nudges something gluey and warm. Recoiling, she flicks on the flashlight and aims it at her feet. A gutted animal lies spread-eagled in a pool of congealing blood, its severed tail protruding from its open mouth. Sobbing, Maddy drops the flashlight and retches into the kitchen sink. "Boots!" she gasps between spasms. "Oh my God!"

A soft chuckle behind her causes her to wheel, her hand across her mouth. She fixes on a dark shape that seems to materialize from the shadows in the corner of the room.

"Get away," she growls. Her own voice is alien, her arms leaden. With tremendous effort, she fights off vertigo and wrenches herself back to the moment. "What do you want?"

Taking a step forward, Cap laughs. "The blood was here, the blood was there, the blood was all around," he chants, enjoying her terror.

Maddy retreats until her back is against the refrigerator. "How did you get in?"

The man hesitates, then laughs again. "Easy," he says, "if you've glazed as many greenhouses as I have."

Quickly, Madelyn pulls open the refrigerator door, holding it before her like a shield. In the dim light cast by the 40 watt bulb, she can see the man in black. Despite the beard, she recognizes him—Cory Neale, in whose left ear winks her zirconium earring.

"All you need is one of these," he says, holding up a steel-handled tool. "And one of these." From his pocket he pulls a gun and levels it at her head.

He's going to kill me. This time I'm going to die.

Maddy closes her eyes, listening for the click of the trigger, waiting for the bullet to rip through her flesh. A surge of regret washes over her. Never to see Jessica or David or Wynn again. Never to walk on the beach or photograph a sunset or listen to Brahms. Tears spring to her eyes. Never again to hear Adam's voice.

"Bang," he says, pulling the trigger. A plastic dart slams into the refrigerator door, held in place by its suction tip. In shock and disbelief, she clings to the metal door like a person drowning. Not a real gun, her muddled senses reassure her, just a toy, a plastic lookalike. Then it hits her.

My god! While I was talking to Wynn, this monster was holding the glass in place with a suction tip dart and cutting through one of the downstairs windows!

Madelyn forces herself to breathe. She watches his eyes assess the room—the stack of drinking glasses, the camera, the brass chain across the kitchen door—and flushes, thinking how pathetic these precautions must seem.

"You and me, we got unfinished business." He takes another step forward in the muted light—a mistake, for in that moment her photographer's eye notices what a less astute observer might overlook: Despite his air of control, he is nervous, jittery. Wet half-moons stain the armpits of his black sweatshirt; his forehead glistens with sweat. He shifts from foot to foot like a child with a full bladder or a person in pain. And in that instant it becomes clear to her what she must do.

"Okay, Cory," she says, feigning a calm she does not feel. "Let's talk. Just like old times." She flicks on the light over the kitchen table, pulls out a chair, and sits, her back to the bloody horror in front of the stove.

His eyes narrow. "Where's the guy?"

"Guy?"

"Don't fuck with me," he growls, drawing a switchblade from his pocket and tripping the spring. The same knife, Maddy sees, nearly gagging in terror. The one he held to her throat in the garage on Willow Drive. He is

SUSAN B. JOHNSON

pacing now, circling the room. "The guy with the boat."

Red and yellow lights flicker behind her eyes as the room slowly begins to rotate, and suddenly she can't breathe, can't focus her mind. But she knows that to save Jessica, she must struggle for consciousness. Act now! screams a voice inside, or Jessie dies! Fueled by rage, she suppresses her panic and forces order upon her chaotic thoughts.

"On his way back from Jacksonville," she says looking at her watch. "Should be here any time." An absurd thought surfaces: *My mother's ship docked in Miami three hours ago.*

In one swift movement, he steps behind her and yanks her head back by the hair, pressing his blade against the taut flesh of her neck.

"I said don't fuck with me."

Her eyes squeezed shut, Maddy smells him—worse than manure this time. A fetid animal odor heightened by—what? Insanity? Drugs? She feels her pulse throbbing like an invitation to the cold steel of his knife blade and tries not to imagine the pain of it slicing across her jugular, tries not to picture what horrors await Jessica, sedated and sleeping in the back bedroom.

Suddenly he releases her. "Not yet," he says with a chuckle. "First we gonna have some fun." With one sudden

284

movement, he jerks her to her feet and rips open the front of her night gown, exposing her left shoulder and the ridge of scar tissue where her breast used to be. Maddy cries out, clutching the shredded cloth, choking back tears of rage and humiliation.

"You ain't no woman, Sister." He bobs and sways before her, rubbing a nervous hand up and down his thigh. "You with your 'Hail Marys' and your 'Holy ghost,'" he barks. "You ain't no woman, you're a fucking freak."

Maddy backs toward the living room door, a noose of hopelessness tightening around her neck. Warily, she watches him duck and shift, his breathing labored, his shoulders tensed. She tries to see behind the madness and discern the lunacy of his intent. Oddly, he is no longer sweating. Instead his eyes have turned glassy, his face flushed. Spittle glistens at the corners of his mouth. Like Ringo, she thinks.

Please don't let them have him, Mama. I'll take care of him. I'll make him better.

You mustn't go near him, Madelyn. Mad dogs sometimes bite.

When he pulls a coil of clothesline from the pouch of his sweatshirt, Maddy lunges for the fireplace poker, but a quick chop with the edge of his hand brings her to her knees.

"An Army buddy taught me that," he says, grinning

down at her. "I learned good." He leans closer. "And you know what else I learned?" When she doesn't answer, he nudges her with the toe of his boot.

Something snaps in Madelyn's brain, a violent rupture that propels her upward, a murderous surge spewing from her solar plexus. She remembers what she hadn't known she knew: his vicious pummeling of her face that night in the garage, the searing pain in her side as he kicked her again and again with his heavy boots. With a roar of fury, she rushes at him, clawing at his eyes, the flesh of his face.

In her rage, she barely hears his howl of pain as they crash to the floor, toppling a lamp and shattering its globe. The enormity of her wrath consumes her, filling the darkness and inuring her to the blows to her head, to the upward thrust of his knee in her groin. But when he wrenches her left arm behind her back and upward, she cries out in agony.

Like a supplicant she goes down on one knee, gasping in pain as he loops the rope around her left wrist. Instinct tells her to fall forward and roll, to kick out in defense, to do whatever she must to keep her right hand free. And for a split second she succeeds. But he quickly overpowers her, immobilizing her on her back. By straddling her and pinning her left wrist with his knee, he frees both his hands to capture and loop her right wrist. Then with a grin of triumph, he binds both wrists together in front, jerking the knot tight and cutting away the extra line. Only then does she begin to accept the hopelessness of her struggle.

"Answer my question, Sister Henry," he pants, sitting astride her battered body. Through angry tears, she sees his eyes jittering in his raked and bleeding face. He yanks her bound hands above her head, pinning them to the floor. "Know what else I learned?"

He forms a loop in the leftover line, his sweat dripping on the thin fabric of her gown. "You always talking about saving my soul," he says. "Always telling me to pray to God to save my soul. Then you put me in the dark, remember? You put me in the dark on my knees, and I learned good then too. What I learned, Sister Henry, is what I'm about to teach you." He makes a loop in the line. "It's what Mama taught me with the handle of the toilet plunger when I was seven and what Booger Mendel taught me in the showers at Hell House. It's what I learned from you that time in the boiler room with your whip and your fucking crucifix!"

Horrified, Maddy fights against the restraints. "No!" she cries. "Cory, it's me, Madelyn Ives!"

He shudders violently. "Need some shit," he mutters, panning the room, his eyes twitching erratically.

"Remember how you used to come over to my house after school?"

"Gotta get some shit," he growls. For a moment, his distraction gives Madelyn hope of getting through to him, talking him down. But before she can formulate a thought, he shifts his weight, loops her ankles, and quickly draws tight the line.

"No, Cory!" she cries, kicking out at his groin with both feet. With a bellow of rage, he slams his fist into her head, leaving her momentarily stunned, tasting blood. She shakes her head to clear her distorted vision, then regrets it, for what she sees quadruples her fright: Behind him Jessica stands blinking in the doorway, her tanned feet bare beneath the white nightgown.

"Mom?" she says in drugged confusion.

"Hoo-wee!" he crows. "Looky what we have here." As she turns to run, he lunges at her like an animal, whipping her head back with a fistful of hair. Jessie screams, clawing at the hand that controls her.

"Let her go, you bastard," screams Madelyn, fighting to free herself. But the knots hold fast.

He kicks at the backs of Jessica's legs forcing her to her knees, his fingers still entangled in her hair. "You with your rich friends and your fancy house," he snarls. "And I'm supposed to be grateful for a few bucks and some castoff clothes?" His voice rises. "I'm supposed to like being laughed at and called "Orphan Annie" and talked to like I'm stupid? Well, look who's in charge now!"

Holding the point of the knife beneath her ear, he wrestles Jessica face down on the floor and straddles her. Then he quickly secures her hands behind her with the fallen lamp cord, using the remainder of the rope to tie one ankle to the table leg and the other to the knob of the front door.

While her daughter lies spread-eagled and sobbing, Madelyn works frantically to loosen the knot at her wrists with her teeth. She watches him pull his sodden sweatshirt over his head, but when she hears the sound of a zipper, she freezes, a red rage rising in her throat. I'll die before I let this happen to her, she thinks, certain that the next few minutes will be her last on earth. As he hoists her hysterical daughter's gown and gropes her with rough fingers, Maddy hunches toward the fireplace, still gnawing at her bonds.

"I'll kill you," screams Jessica, writhing in rage and whipping her head from side to side. As he reaches out to grab her hair, she catches his little finger in her teeth and bites down hard.

He howls like an animal as her teeth cut to bone, and, frantic to free himself, he slams her head over and over against the floor, then rears back on his knees to look at his half-severed finger. Swearing and bleeding, he struggles to his feet, his pants around his knees. In his pain and the dim light, he has forgotten Madelyn, doesn't see her grip the hatchet with both bound hands, lift it above her head, and hurl it with all her might, its trajectory true, its sharpened blade seeking the mark. He grunts as the blow drives him backwards to the wall where, for a moment, he hangs, his eyes wide with surprise. Then he slumps like a rag doll, the axe blade buried in the flesh of his abdomen.

Through the darkness she swims, toward the moonlight, up to the place where Jessica calls, "Mom, Mom." As she breaks the surface, she feels her body convulse in protest at the pain that sears through her back and shoulder. She curls inward, drawing up her knees beneath the quilt and turns her face into the crook of her arm.

Someone places a cool cloth on her forehead as she tries to open her eyes, but her mind swirls in confusion. Why is she lying on the floor? And who is that person asleep beneath the blanket just over there? The room swarms with men talking, shifting furniture. One of them leans over the sleeper and lifts the blanket, revealing blood—lots of blood—and a man with black hair. Not David. Adam?

"The police have come, Mom," Jessica says. "And

the ambulance is on its way from Chiefland. Should be here in about twenty minutes." Maddy feels her daughter's soft breath near her ear and is comforted.

"Ambulance?" Her mouth has trouble forming the word.

"Here's some water." With trembling hands, Jessica slips a drinking straw between Maddy's lips, but she can't drink lying on this hard surface and struggles to turn, to sit up. "What happened?" she asks in somebody else's voice.

"Sh-h-h" says Jessica. "Just lie still."

But the braided rug reminds her of something she is supposed to do, an urgent mission, something about—
"Boots!" she cries, straining to see in the swirling lights.

"It's gone, Mom," Jessie says, her teeth chattering. "They took it away."

Maddy begins to cry, remembering the cat's mutilated body, the staring yellow eyes. Who would hurt Boots?

Ben Waite's large, warm hand grasps hers. "You're a remarkable woman, Madelyn Ives." She studies the dark granite of his face, sculpted with anger and shadows. "And I'm very much in your debt."

In that moment the tide turns, and all the terror comes flooding back. *The man in black was here— Cory Neale, with his blunt-handled glass cutter and his— Mustn't cry out, mustn't let him hurt—*

291

"Jessie?" she says, straining toward her daughter's face. "Jessie?"

"I'm okay, Mom. We're both gonna be okay." Maddy feels the cool of the damp cloth on her face and tries to organize her thoughts. She wants to ask questions, but Jessica shakes her dark curls and whispers to her like a child. "He can't hurt us anymore, Mom. Cory's gone." Following her daughter's eyes toward the sleeper lying a few feet away, she feels his awful stillness. His whole body—even his head—is completely covered with what she now recognizes as the lavender blanket from Anna Hayes' bed.

Her own head throbs, despite the pillow beneath it, and a spasm of pain sears through her shoulder. She recoils from the sudden flash of a camera as one of the police officers pans the room taking digital photographs. In rapid succession, he shoots a shattered lamp in the corner, a length of rope knotted around a table leg, and the safety chain on the kitchen door. Bad composition, she thinks. Not enough back lighting. Too many shadows.

An eerie wail rises above the drone of men's voices. Someone is in torment, she thinks, then realizes the sound comes from her own throat. For the photographer has removed Anna Hayes' blanket and is discharging his flash over and over at the grisly thing that lies beneath.

"For God's sake, Ramirez!" yells Ben, kneeling beside Maddy to block her view. But he is too late. She has already caught sight of the horror that was once Cory Neale, a slaughtered animal with a severed hepatic artery still oozing blood.

With a sob, Madelyn draws her knees beneath her and begins to crawl away, her stomach heaving with pain and shock and revulsion. "I killed him!" she gasps between spasms. "My God, I killed Cory Neale!"

But Ben's strong hands catch her, fend off her feeble protests, pull her close, and hold her firmly.

"You did what you had to do, Madelyn," he says evenly. "You saved your daughter."

Imprisoned against Ben's warmth, she feels her body go limp and empties her tired mind. *I can't fight anymore. Can't fix this horrible thing that's happened.* Ben rocks her like a baby, holding a shawl around her shoulders and his hand across her eyes. Little by little, she feels the world begin to right itself again. Within the cocoon of his arms, Madelyn's breathing steadies, her pounding pulse subsides. When at last he releases her, Cory's corpse has disappeared.

"Tell me what you know," she says. She pushes into a sitting position and meets Ben's eyes.

"Not now," he says. "When you're stronger."

"Now," says Maddy. "All of it."

Ben crouches before her, searching for the words. "Apparently, he cut the telephone wires while you were in the middle of a conversation with your friend in Ohio."

"Wynn."

"Right. Well, she got scared and called the station. The night clerk alerted me, and I contacted Ramirez on lookout down the street." He wipes his forehead with his sleeve—his pajama sleeve, Maddy realizes for the first time. "When Ramirez checked around, he discovered the laundry room glass missing, heard sounds of a struggle, and radioed for backup. By the time we got in, it was over. The man was already near death." For a moment, he lowers his chin to his chest, then meets her gaze with tired eyes. "He must have come up from the beach," he says. "I'm sorry, Madelyn. Really, truly sorry."

She shudders involuntarily.

"From the looks of things, you put up one hell of a fight," he says. "You saw him attacking Jessica and sprang into action like some kind of enraged Apache warrior." Wonder and admiration resonate in his voice. "Takes a lot of skill to hurl a hand axe," he says. "You nailed that bastard from ten feet away." He shakes his head in awe. "Now where in hell did a school teacher from Ohio learn to do a thing like that?"

Chapter 29
Tuesday, January 6

Muted voices on the other side of the curtain—one groggy, one bright and businesslike—remind Maddy that this room is not hers alone. She folds back the coarse hospital sheet and elevates the head of her bed with the control, careful not to jostle her bandaged shoulder.

So many flowers. Daisies from Wynn, who knows her weakness. A hand-potted herb basket from Fee. Beside a huge white poinsettia from the Jacobys sits a tiny African violet from Jessica. And from Adam, roses and roses and roses.

With her good arm, she reaches for her reading glasses and unfolds his letter for the fifth time

January 3

Dear M,

For the past two days I've been searching for

SUSAN B. JOHNSON

the right word to express how I feel. Grateful, first and foremost, that you're alive, but that word by itself doesn't do the job. How about euphoric? lucky? hungry?

Now I'm starting to think maybe it's a noun I need. Admiration? Awe?

Yesterday I sat by the ocean in my wheelchair, which I loathe, questioning the self-abnegation that cost me the last twenty-two years with you. The only explanation is that I felt unworthy in the light of all your goodness (bravery? decency?).

I want to tear off this cast and run all the way to Cypress Key. I want to taste your mouth and breathe in the perfume of you and bury my face in your hair. I want to grab hold of you and hang on for the rest of my life.

And just as I'm about to dismiss words for the paltry, inadequate shams they are, the perfect one appears—shimmering and resplendent in all its complex simplicity.

The word is *love*, Maddy McCandless. I love you, love you, love you.

Even the fifth reading causes her throat to constrict.

Maddy smiles painfully, her jaw still bruised. She examines her face in her hand mirror. Not too awful. A couple of yellowish bruises on her forehead, a scabbed-over scrape on her chin.

Beneath Adam's letter is a note from David, whose trans-Atlantic flight will land at Kennedy in exactly two hours and twenty-three minutes. Maddy pulls the sheet of heavy cream stationery from its Kohl & Sumner envelope and studies the slant of David's script. What would a handwriting analyst read in that bold capital "C"? Self-confidence? Egotism? She imagines him writing those two words with his Mont Blanc ballpoint, his blond head bent to the task, and a rush of tenderness wells unbidden in her throat. "Come home," is all it says.

Maddy places the two envelopes side by side on her tray table. Two men, each attractive in his own way. Together she and David have a rich if imperfect history. Yet she and Adam—

Her thoughts are interrupted by the ring of the telephone on the table beside her bed.

"Your phone's fixed," says Jessica.

"Good. Has anyone called?"

"Only Mrs. Orbison. She's picking me up in twenty minutes. We should be there by ten o'clock."

"Fee," says Maddy. "Call her Fee."

"Whatever. Anyway, we need to arrive at the

Gainesville airport no later than noon. By the way, the airfare was quite a bit more than you estimated. How do you feel?"

"Sore, but ambulatory."

"Anything you need?"

Need? For a moment the question overwhelms her. Serenity, she thinks. And time, emptied of terror. And love. But whose? David's or Adam's?

"No thanks, honey. Just get me out of here."

"Done," says Jessica.

Maddy listens to the dial tone for a moment, then returns the receiver to its cradle. A new inflection rings in her daughter's voice, a crisp efficiency suggesting plans to implement and goals to meet. Don't get your hopes up, she cautions herself. You know the game.

She glances at her watch, then eases her feet to the floor, assessing her discomfort. Better, today, she decides. No more searing pain when she moves, just a dull ache in her back and shoulder.

"Listen to your body," the doctor had instructed. "It'll tell you when it's had enough." And since today is good-bye day, staying in bed is not an option.

She draws the canvas carryall from her narrow closet and inspects its contents. Sweats, Jessie has packed. Clean underwear. A soft cotton cardigan. Sandals. And at the bottom sits her cosmetic case and hair brush. She showers, dresses with the help of a nurse, then goes to work on her face.

By ten o'clock she has packed her few belongings and transferred the huge vase of roses to her sleeping roommate's side of the curtain. She gives the room a final inspection, then heads for the elevator clutching Wynn's daisies in her good right arm.

Crossing the main lobby, Maddy smiles at the sight of Fee's old Volvo double parked beyond the glass doors, its emergency blinkers flashing. At the sight of her, Fee lunges from the car, arms outstretched, remembering just in time her friend's bruised ribs. Instead the two friends air kiss, then laugh at the artifice.

"Look at you!" Fee says. "Jess and I were expecting a wheelchair."

"I sneaked past the nurses' station and escaped," grins Maddy. "Get me the hell out of here."

All the way to the airport, Fee regales them with stories of her Aruba holiday—of dining aboard the 110 foot yacht *La Niña* courtesy of Spain's King Juan Carlos, who was enjoying an extended cruise; of photographing, from the ship's helicopter, the earthquake damage to Haiti.

"Looking at it on TV just doesn't give you the true picture," she says with a shudder. "Terrible! When you see it from above, you're amazed that *anybody* escaped alive."

Madelyn is grateful to Fee for distracting her from the anxiety of a second farewell. One down, two to go, she thinks. But will David be number three? Will Adam? In no time at all, Fee pulls to the curb in Delta's off-loading lane, and a skycap steps forward to accept the luggage.

David or Adam? Adam or David?

You can do this, Maddy tells herself. You're tougher than you think.

In the chill of evening, she sits on the deck wrapped in a quilt on the old redwood chaise, listening to a Great Horned Owl interrogate the moon. Her head throbs, partly from the damage to her jaw but mostly from the strain of the past eight hours. Saying goodbye with grace had required enormous effort.

She hadn't managed it a year and a half ago when Jessie stormed from the house threatening never to return. Instead she had lost fifteen pounds in three weeks from anxiety and nausea.

Nor had she handled David's departure well last September, crying and crying until she lost her voice, necessitating a nine-day medical leave of absence. His desertion had also added $55 to her monthly expenses—$15 for sleep-inducing sedatives and $40 to touch up her sudden streak of gray.

But just now, as a scrim of clouds draws across the moon, she congratulates herself on mastering the art of graceful parting. This morning, for example, before going down to the hospital lobby to meet Fee, she had taken the elevator to the fourth floor and rapped softly before pushing open the door of room 402.

Like her own hospital room, this one had two beds, but only one was occupied. By a child, Maddy thought crazily. A brown raisin of a child.

In her own element, Minneola Jones stood steadfast and indomitable by the sheer power of her knowledge. Maddy recalls how, at their first meeting, the woman's black eyes had pierced her own veil of equanimity, exposing her fear of the man pursuing her. "Ooo, chile, you got the look!" Minneola had pronounced. At the time, only she knew what she meant.

But in room 402, diminished by the bright yellow walls, the expanse of sterile bed linen, she lay curled like a small, brown animal plucked from its familiar woodlands and caged into submissiveness.

Maddy had tiptoed to the bedside and taken Minneola's hand into her own. At her touch, the old woman roused.

"It's you," she said in a voice froggy with disuse. She had licked her parched lips and struggled to sit. But the effort was too great, and she sank into the pillow with a sigh.

"Yes," said Madelyn, pouring water from a carafe. She thrust her good arm beneath the fragile shoulders and held the glass to Minneola's lips. A bird, she remembered thinking. No more than eighty pounds. "Look," she said, "daisies."

But Minneola had no interest in flowers; her gaze was riveted on Madelyn's face. "So," she said nodding, "he finally come."

"Yes, but now he's gone. Forever."

Minneola nodded and closed her eyes. "Then it's time to let go, chile. Time to let go." Her claw-like fingers clutched the fold of the sheet, drawing it to her chin. Maddy had sat rigidly in the bedside chair, watching the old woman's breathing settle into the rhythm of sleep. Finally, she rose and started for the door on tiptoe, almost forgetting. At the last moment she returned, slipped from her wrist Minneola's talisman of whitened bone, and pressed it into the old woman's hand.

"Thank you, my friend," she whispered. She had not cried when she bent to kiss the withered cheek. Instead she had walked, dry-eyed, down the corridor to the bank of elevators.

But that wasn't all. She had kept her composure at the airport, too. A chill breeze lifts the hair on Maddy's forehead, and she hugs the quilt to her body. Closing her eyes, she pictures Jessie's expression as she started down the Delta boarding ramp. Determined, apprehensive, committed. But if the decision to enroll at OSU had not been easy, at least it had been Jessie's own. Will she follow through? Maddy wonders. Only time will tell.

As she tucks her feet beneath the coverlet, she permits herself a moment of grief, wishing for the furry bulk of Boots to warm her toes. But she quickly shakes the thought away. I'll change what I can, she thinks, and learn to accept the rest. Her thoughts turn to the choice that looms before her.

Despite the brevity of David's note, she understands that he wants to give their marriage another chance, and part of her longs for the same. Her new independence has not kept her from missing the rhythms of marriage and the comfort of couplehood. David needs her warmth, her sense of fun, to lend balance to his intensity. And in exchange he offers her security and quiet love.

Adam, on the other hand, needs her spirit and her intellect to complement his own. For these he offers laughter, adventure, and a certain reckless love.

Which will it be—Adam or David? Sails or an anchor?

"Wh-who," calls the Great Horned Owl across the darkness.

SUSAN B. JOHNSON

Who, indeed?

The answer, when it presents itself, appears brilliant and clear as if written in stars across the night sky. In this new year it isn't what David needs or Adam wants that matters anymore. Now it's time for what *she* needs—to listen to her conscience and resign from Harding College.

She'll miss her students and her colleagues but not the grind of writing endless reports, grading stacks of student essays, and avoiding touchy-feely with Dr. Friedman.

It's time to listen to Wynn, who has offered to sell Anna Hayes' cottage to her for half what it's worth—unless, as Wynn fears, the echo of violence still resonates within its walls. But that was then, as Jessie would say. Maddy is confident any lingering ghosts can be exorcised with lots of fresh air and hard work.

It's time to listen to Fee, who knows of a small photographer's studio available for sub-let down on the strand and a good psychiatrist to guide her through the maze of healing. She hopes David will insist on counseling for Jessica as well.

Maddy realizes with surprise that Jessie and David are no longer her first priority, and she pauses to test this truth with the litmus of her conscience. No guilt, no rancor, no nagging sense of loss. Only a sweet rush of release. The hatchet buried in Cory Neale's body marked the end of not one life, but two: The old Madelyn Ives, tentative and dependent, no longer exists.

And Adam? Instinctively, she reaches into her pocket for her cigarettes, then crumples the pack in disgust. Although Adam loves her, his passion is the sea. She smiles remembering the night they spent together, hearing again the question she hadn't been prepared to answer.

Why can't we just love each other, Mad—here and now, without the impediment of promises?

No, she decides, not here and now. Not yet. First I need to deal with all that's happened and relearn the joy of solitude. I need to think and plan and savor my hard-won independence and strength. Best of all I need to explore my talent as an artist. And that, my love, takes time.

Besides, you have an appointment in Tobago.

As channel markers wink and beckon out on the dark gulf, she breathes deeply of the salt-scented air. The tide is in full flood now, curling halfway up the beach. She holds perfectly still, listening to the whisper of the surf as it surges forward, recedes, then rushes toward her again.

With a welling joy, Maddy casts the quilt aside, ignores her battered body, and strides across the sand, opening her arms to the night wind.

Once again Minneola is right. It's time to "let go, chile. Just let go."

About the author:

Susan B. Johnson is a novelist, playwright, journalist, and historian. Her play *Finders Weepers* was published in 1993 and has been performed in venues across the country. Her short stories, columns, and articles have appeared in many national and regional publications. In 2008 both a nonfiction book, *Savannah's Little Crooked Houses: If These Walls Could Talk,* and a novel, *Spirit Willing: A Savannah Haunting,* were published, for which she was nominated Georgia Author of the Year.

Susan lives in a 215-year-old cottage in the historic heart of Savannah, Georgia. For seventeen years she taught composition and literature at both Armstrong State University and South University in Savannah. During those years she wrote newspaper columns and magazine articles for various publications. Now retired, she devotes her time to writing and watercolor painting. You can view her artwork on her website: www.susanbjohnson.com.

OTHER BOOKS BY SUSAN B. JOHNSON

Spirit Willing: A Savannah Haunting (Fiction)

Savannah's Little Crooked Houses: If These Walls Could Talk (Non-fiction)

Sean's Yawn (Illustrated Children's Book)

Made in the USA
Lexington, KY
18 February 2017